They made a mess.
Now he's taking
out the trash.

CLEAN SWEEP

The Keepers of Warden's Rest
Episode one

JEREMY FABIANO

CLEAN SWEEP

EPISODE ONE

THE KEEPERS OF WARDEN'S REST

JEREMY FABIANO

CLEAN SWEEP
The Keepers of Warden's Rest Episode One

JEREMY FABIANO

Copyright © 2025, by Jeremy Fabiano
All rights reserved.

This is a work of fiction. Any resemblance to reality is coincidental.

No part of this book may be reproduced in any form or by any electronic or mechanical means, including information storage and retrieval systems, without written permission from the author, except for the use of brief quotations in a book review.

www.jeremyfabianoauthor.com

Cover design by Jacqueline Sweet Design

Also by Jeremy Fabiano

The Aetheric Codex

- The Clockwork Heart
- The Lost Pages
- Shadows of Gearford
- The Forgotten City
- The Forbidden Spell (*Coming Soon*)

The Keepers of Warden's Rest

- Clean Sweep
- Field Tripped (*Coming Soon*)

The Tempest Chronicles

- A Fable of Magic
- Necromancer's Bane
- The Queen's Gambit
- Hour of Reckoning
- The Stones of Hygeia
- Trials of the Firstborn
- Risen By War

Precipice To War

- Bishop's Gambit Omnibus (Precipice Book 1)

Omnibus Editions

The Tempest Chronicles Omnibus 1 (Books 1-3)

The Tempest Chronicles Omnibus 2 (Books 4-6)

To my family, my friends, my Inner Circle of author friends and two puppers and two kitties that left us too early.

Thank you for all of your love and support.

"And it is my sincere hope," he added, "that we can all look forward to what Warden's Rest will accomplish in the coming years. This place—this school—has produced more heroes in one night than I've seen in a decade of courtly pretense."

Before Alden could process that, the Archduke turned to the Dean. "And as for Mr. Voss..."

Alden's eyes narrowed. "I'm good, thanks."

-Archduke Rendell Valcroft & Alden Voss

CHAPTER ONE

Alden Voss pushed the mop bucket forward, its worn wheels rattling against the stone floor. A slow, deliberate pace. No rush. He knew what was waiting for him behind the restroom door.

The noise inside made it obvious. A muffled grunt. A sharp intake of breath. The slap of a hand hitting tile. Every damn year, some kid thought he was the toughest bastard in Warden's Rest Academy. Every damn year, that same type of kid found some poor scrawny first-year to prove it on.

Alden sighed, shoved the door open, and rolled the mop bucket inside.

It was exactly what he expected.

The restroom reeked of cheap cologne and bad decisions. Three students stood near the sinks, watching like spectators at a pit fight. One of them—a wiry kid, red in the face and gasping—was shoved against the wall. The other, built like he'd been raised on raw steak and bad manners, had a fistful of the kid's tunic.

No magic. No enchanted gauntlets or arcane circles. Just a bigger kid throwing his weight around because he could.

The bully didn't stop when Alden entered.

That was a mistake.

Alden pulled the mop from its bucket and let the head drip onto the tile. He was too old for speeches. Too tired for lectures. So he simply walked forward, boots scuffing against the wet floor, and stared at the bigger kid until the pressure alone forced him to turn.

The bully let go of the scrawny kid and squared up. Smug grin, cocky stance.

He's gotten away with this too many times before. Probably figures a janitor wasn't worth his time. Alden rested the mop against his shoulder. "You finished?"

The bully rolled his shoulders. "What's it to you, old man?"

Alden ignored the insult. His eyes flicked to the kid who'd been shoved against the wall. *He's still standing, at least. Good.* "Get out of here, kid."

The boy hesitated, shooting a glance at his tormentor.

Alden took a step closer. "I said—"

THE KID BOLTED.

The three spectators suddenly decided they had places to be, slipping out the door without a word. That left just Alden and the bully, standing in a room full of damp tile and bad energy.

The kid—no, scratch that—the *idiot*—didn't back down. If anything, he squared his shoulders. "I don't take orders from a damn janitor."

Alden dunked the mop back in the bucket, swirled it around, and lifted it. Cold, soapy water dripped from the head. He raised it to the kid's face, close enough for him to smell the industrial-grade cleanser. "Tell me," Alden said, voice flat, "you ever get to know the business-end of a mop?"

The kid froze.

A single drop of dirty water rolled off the mop head and splattered against the tile.

Alden waited. No words. Just the quiet drip of a mop held at eye level.

The kid's jaw worked. His hands clenched, then relaxed. He stepped back. "Whatever." A poor attempt at nonchalance. "Not worth my time."

Alden kept the mop up until the kid turned and walked out. When the door swung shut, he exhaled, setting the mop back in the bucket.

I'm getting too damned old for this.

Alden took his time mopping. The floor wasn't even dirty, but the slow repetition of movement gave him a moment to clear his thoughts. This job, as simple as it was, had its advantages.

Nobody expected anything from him.

Nobody asked him for favors.

Nobody called him "Centurion."

Most of the students didn't even know his name, and that suited him just fine.

The paycheck wasn't much, but it was enough to keep him fed. And tonight, there was something worth looking forward to.

Hugo Crevane's Void-Crusted Steak.

Alden had been here long enough to know the school's kitchen served up some strange things. Half the time, the food glowed. Sometimes it hummed with residual magic. On rare occasions, it tried to escape the plate entirely.

But Crevane's steak? No…That was different.

That was perfection.

Aged in a gravity pocket, seared over ethereal blue flames, and seasoned with spices that probably weren't technically legal. The kind of meal you only got once a year. The kind that made an old soldier forget about war, about the past, about anything other than the taste of something that good.

It was the one thing he gave a damn about.

Alden finished mopping, wrung out the head, and gave the

restroom a final glance. Spotless and quiet again. He sighed, grabbed the mop bucket, and headed out.

Tonight would be peaceful.

He'd finish his rounds for the day, grab a plate, and enjoy a damn good steak.

Nothing was going to ruin that.

Alden had barely made it three steps out of the restroom when the walls thrummed with a low resonance, and a disembodied voice rang out across the academy, clear as if the speaker was standing right behind him.

"All staff members, please report to the staff lounge immediately. Repeat, all staff members to the staff lounge."

Alden stopped in his tracks, closed his eyes, and let out a long, slow exhale through his nose.

He knew that tone. That clipped, official voice that meant someone needed something, and somehow, he was going to get dragged into it.

He could already hear the conversation. "Alden, we need a favor." "Alden, since you're already walking around the halls..." "Alden, can you just handle this one thing?"

Nope. Not tonight. Tonight, I have a once-in-a-year date with perfection.

He grumbled under his breath, yanked the mop bucket harder than necessary, and turned down the hall toward the lounge.

Whatever it was, it better be quick.

CHAPTER TWO

Alden had put away the mop, stowed the bucket, and washed his hands before making his way to the staff lounge. The door stood open, spilling the low murmur of conversation into the hall. He stepped inside and found a smaller gathering than usual—Four teachers, clustered near the center of the room, exchanging quiet, uncertain looks.

At the front, standing with a commanding posture despite his age, was Dean Albrecht Vayne. The man had the presence of someone who had long since grown used to being obeyed. His robes, deep blue trimmed with gold filigree, were pristine despite his many years, and his eyes—cold, gray, and calculating—swept across the room as if mentally tallying the worth of every individual present.

The hum of conversation died the moment he cleared his throat.

"As you may have noticed, we are short-staffed today." His voice carried effortlessly, filling the lounge without the need for magical amplification. "The senior faculty has been called away on a matter of extreme importance, as per a direct missive from the king himself."

Alden leaned against the back wall, arms crossed. *Ugh. I really don't like the sound of that. Sounds like increased—*

Vayne continued, "This means that the responsibility of overseeing the academy now falls upon our remaining personnel. Orin Hale, Tobin Crane, Milena Star, Evora Nightvale, and Alden Voss will ensure that order is maintained among the students. You will all act as their authority and protection in our absence."

Damn.

Alden stiffened and he uncrossed his arms. He shoved his hands into his pockets before they curled into fists.

"Wait," he said, slow and deliberate, as if testing the words before letting them out, "you're telling me that every single senior professor—every battle-hardened spellcaster, warlock, and scholar in this school—just packed up and left?"

Dean Vayne's expression remained unreadable. "That is correct."

"To deal with what, exactly?"

Vayne paused just a second too long. "A classified matter."

Alden frowned. "And what, pray tell, are we protecting the students *from*?"

"That is *also* a classified matter."

Alden let out a humorless chuckle, shaking his head. "Of course it is."

Vayne folded his hands behind his back, tilting his head just slightly. "You, of all people, should understand, Mr. Voss. A soldier *follows orders*, regardless of whether he understands them or agrees with them. Duty is not a matter of convenience. It is a commitment. You swore that oath once, did you not?"

Alden's jaw tightened.

He knew exactly what the old man was doing. It was the same tone commanders had used on him years ago. Duty. Service. The weight of expectation, pressing down like iron shackles.

His gut told him something was wrong about this.

But his brain was tired of arguing and told him it didn't matter.

Alden exhaled slowly, nodded once, and grumbled something unintelligible under his breath.

The Dean took that as acceptance.

"Then that settles it. You all have your assignments. See that the students behave."

Alden rolled his shoulders, already regretting not pushing back harder. Nothing ever went right when the chain of command started keeping secrets.

The meeting ended with little fanfare. The teachers filtered out in quiet groups, murmuring among themselves. Alden made no effort to keep up. He wasn't one of them, and he knew it.

"Unbelievable," he muttered, running a hand down his face as he walked toward the exit.

The other four teachers had already gathered near the hallway outside the lounge. Tobin Crane—the closest thing this skeleton crew had to an actual combat expert besides himself—was speaking in low tones to Milena Star and Orin Hale. Evora Nightvale, meanwhile, stood slightly apart from the others, arms folded, watching Alden approach.

"Try not to look so thrilled," she said dryly.

"Hard to be thrilled when the entire senior staff vanishes on the king's orders and leaves us with babysitting duty," Alden replied.

Orin glanced toward the lounge, as if expecting the Dean to be standing there. "I won't pretend this isn't... strange. The king's summons—the way they left in such a hurry. None of this feels right."

"Feels like a bad joke," Tobin muttered. "There aren't enough of us. Not for this many students."

Alden grunted. "Wouldn't be enough even if we were. You think these kids give a damn about authority figures when half of them can shoot fire from their hands?"

Milena exhaled sharply. "We're not supposed to fight them, Alden. We're supposed to keep them *safe*."

Aldens scoffed. "Safe from what, exactly?"

Another pause.

That's what bothers me the most. Not the fact that the teachers had been left behind. Not the fact that this was probably a setup for something worse. No, what really *makes my skin crawl was that none of us actually knew what they were supposed to be guarding against.* He didn't bother voicing his opinion—it'd be wasted on them.

Orin exhaled through his nose, arms folding. "This isn't about precaution. If it was, the Dean wouldn't have dragged all of us in like it was an emergency. He'd have just let the normal staff rotation handle things. No, this feels like a distraction—like whatever's happening, we were never meant to be a part of it."

"Maybe," Alden said. He didn't believe it.

Evora studied him with quiet scrutiny, her gaze sharper than the others. "You don't trust the Dean's claims," she said. It wasn't a question.

Alden met her stare, weighing his words. "I don't trust a lot of things. But I especially don't trust being told to sit and wait when I don't know what I'm waiting for."

Evora didn't argue.

None of them did.

Tobin finally let out a sigh, rubbing the bridge of his nose. "Well. Until we get more information, our job is still the same." He shifted, glancing toward Alden. "I imagine you're going to keep your usual routine?"

Alden shrugged. "If it means not having to listen to students whining, yeah."

Tobin smirked. "Glad to see you're embracing the role."

"Don't push your luck," Alden grumbled, already turning toward the hallway.

He needed air.

The feeling in his gut wasn't going away.

Something is definitely *off. I can* feel *it.*

CHAPTER THREE

Alden made his way toward the janitorial closet, content to let the day pass without further involvement in anyone's problems. That had been the plan, anyway.

Halfway down the hall, he spotted the kid from earlier.

The scrawny one. The one who'd been backed into a corner by that dumb bastard with more muscle than sense. The boy stood in front of a locker, staring at the floor, shoulders hunched like he was trying to fold in on himself.

The bruising around his left eye was fresh.

Alden exhaled through his nose.

Not my problem.

The kid would learn, just like everyone else did. You got knocked down, you either crawled or figured out how to stand back up. The world didn't hand out second chances. That's just the way of things.

Alden had made it two steps past him when he stopped.

Something in his gut twisted—not the kind of twist that warned of danger, just the one that whispered, *You know damn well that's not right.*

He grumbled under his breath and turned back.

"Kid."

The boy flinched and snapped his head up, his wide eyes darting to Alden's before quickly dropping again.

Alden sighed. *Too damn young to already be looking at the floor like that.*

"That bastard get you again after I left?"

The kid hesitated, rubbing at his arm. "Yeah," he muttered.

Alden felt his jaw tighten. He had a pretty good idea how it had played out. The bully waited until Alden was gone, cornered the kid somewhere quieter, and made a point.

Kids nearby chuckled under their breath, not quite quiet enough to avoid notice.

Alden's gaze flicked toward them. They shut up real fast.

He turned back to the boy. "What's your name, kid?"

The kid looked like he wanted to just disappear into his own shoes. "Milo," he mumbled.

Alden nodded. "Milo. You ever think about sticking up for yourself?"

Milo shifted uncomfortably, glancing away.

Yeah. That answered that.

Alden didn't press the issue. "Come talk to me after your next class," he said instead. "I'll be cleaning the stairwells."

Milo hesitated. Uncertainty flickered behind his eyes, like he wasn't sure whether to trust what he was hearing.

Alden wasn't in the business of making speeches, so he just waited.

After a few beats, the kid nodded. Quick. Barely noticeable. Then he bolted down the hall.

Alden shook his head. *Poor kid.*

"You alright, kid?"

The boy flinched at the sound of his voice but didn't look up. "Yeah."

Alden folded his arms, glancing down the hallway. A few

students loitered nearby, pretending not to listen. He caught the faintest snicker from one of them.

His eyes flicked back to him. "That bastard get you again?"

The kid hesitated, then nodded. "Right after you left."

Alden's jaw tightened.

"Why don't you stick up for yourself?"

The kid's fingers curled into his lap, but he didn't answer. The other students nearby chuckled again, though none of them had the balls to say anything outright.

Alden turned his head, fixing them with a slow, deliberate look.

Silence.

Satisfied, he returned his attention to the kid. "What's your name?"

The boy hesitated, then mumbled, "Milo Ferin."

"Alright, Milo." Alden adjusted his stance. "Meet me after your next class. I'll be cleaning the stairwells."

Milo's head snapped up. "What?"

"You heard me."

The kid hesitated, eyes darting between Alden and the hallway, as if waiting for some kind of punchline.

Alden just waited.

After a long pause, Milo nodded—quick, nervous—then grabbed his bag and rushed toward his next class.

Alden shook his head and sighed.

The janitorial closet was exactly as he'd left it. A cramped, dimly lit room filled with buckets, rags, cleaning solvents, and the occasional questionable smell that refused to die no matter how many times he scrubbed the place down with disinfectant.

He grabbed the squeegee, some clean rags and a bucket of water before heading toward the front of the school. The windows were long overdue for a cleaning, and if he didn't get to them soon, some smartass student would enchant a rag to do it, which would almost definitely end in broken glass. *Again.*

He stepped out onto the grand front steps, letting the cool air wash him as he left the building.

Warden's Rest Academy sat atop a sprawling hill, its front gates a good hundred yards away, flanked by towering wrought-iron fences. Beyond that, a long, winding path led toward the city. The academy itself was a masterpiece of stonework and magic. It was a place where architecture and enchantment blended so seamlessly that the walls practically hummed with residual energy.

From where Alden stood at the top of the steps, he could see everything—the front courtyard, the gates, the tree-lined path beyond.

It all looked normal.

So why the hell do I feel like someone is watching me?

The hair on his arms stood up.

That old, familiar feeling. The one he'd thought he'd left behind all those years ago. His body tensed before his mind even registered it—the kind of instinct that didn't fade, no matter how many years passed.

Alden scanned the grounds again.

Nothing seemed out of place. Students moved across the yard, some heading toward classes, others laughing in small groups. The front gates stood still, locked as usual.

But his gut didn't lie.

Someone is watching. Waiting. I can feel it.

He turned back toward the windows, dipping the squeegee into the bucket. His fingers tightened around the handle.

Old habits die hard.

Whatever it was, he'd deal with it when it showed itself.

CHAPTER
FOUR

Alden grabbed a fresh rag, a bucket, and a stiff-bristled brush before locking up the janitorial closet. Cleaning the stairwells wasn't his favorite job, but it gave him an excuse to be away from the rest of the academy for a while. The stone steps leading to the upper halls gathered grime far faster than they should—something about the enchantments embedded in the walls interfered with proper upkeep. He'd long since given up trying to understand it.

By the time he reached the first stairwell, he rolled up his sleeves and got to work.

Scrubbing. Wiping. Repetitive, thoughtless work. The kind he actually liked.

Halfway through, the faint sound of hesitant footsteps echoed behind him.

He didn't turn around.

"I was starting to think you wouldn't show up," he said, dipping the brush into the bucket.

Milo shuffled to a stop near the base of the stairs. "Didn't have anything to lose." His voice was quiet, but there was something flat in the way he said it—like he believed it more than he should.

Alden set the brush down and leaned against the railing. "That a fact?"

Milo shrugged.

Alden watched him for a moment, taking in the way the kid stood just a little too small, like he was always trying to make himself a smaller target. The bruises on his face had darkened since earlier, stark against his pale skin.

"What's your magic?" Alden asked.

Milo hesitated. "It's... nothing."

"Didn't ask if it was useful. Asked what it was."

Milo looked away. His hands fidgeted at his sides before he finally muttered, "I can make things sparkle."

Alden raised an eyebrow. "Sparkle?"

Milo sighed and held out his hand. A faint shimmer of glittering light danced across his fingertips before vanishing. It didn't emit heat, didn't surge with arcane energy. Just... twinkled.

Alden grunted. "That got a name?"

Milo kicked at the floor. "Shining Veil."

Alden considered it. "Sounds fancier than what it does."

"Yeah, well. That's what I get." Milo crossed his arms, voice bitter. "Everyone else gets fire or shields or gravity magic. I get Shining Veil."

Alden nodded slowly. "You'll figure out a use for it someday."

Milo huffed. "Doubt it."

Alden bent to grab the brush again, speaking as he worked. "Nothing's ever truly useless. Just gotta figure out what it's meant for."

Milo let out a short, humorless laugh. "Well, I am—useless, that is."

Alden paused mid-scrub.

Milo scuffed his foot against the stone, staring at the floor. "I'm too puny. Too weak. They know it. I could have fire magic, and they'd still find a way to knock me down."

Alden exhaled through his nose and set the brush aside. *Damn it.* He wasn't supposed to care. Wasn't supposed to get involved.

Yet here he was.

"Come here, kid."

Milo blinked at him. "What?"

"You heard me." Alden straightened, rolling his shoulders. "Since you think you're useless, let's fix that."

Milo hesitated before stepping closer.

Alden studied him, taking in the way he held himself—shoulders tight, hands half-clenched, feet too close together. Not confident. Not ready.

"No magic. No tricks," Alden said. "Just some basics. First thing—balance. You stand like that in a fight, you'll end up on the ground before you throw a punch."

Milo shifted awkwardly. "I don't... throw punches."

Alden snorted. "Yeah. Figured." He stepped forward and nudged Milo's foot with his own. "Widen your stance. Just a little. Keep yourself centered."

Milo obeyed, though he looked unsure.

"Good. Now, hands up." Alden raised his own, demonstrating. "You don't need to swing. Just block. Defend."

Milo copied the movement, stiff and uncertain.

Alden stepped in, slow and deliberate, tapping Milo's arm lightly with the back of his knuckles. "See? You're open. Raise it higher."

Milo adjusted.

Alden tested the kid's stance again, pushing gently against his shoulder. Milo wobbled but didn't fall. That was an improvement.

Alden nodded. "Better."

Milo frowned. "This isn't gonna stop anyone from kicking my ass."

"No," Alden admitted. "Not yet."

Milo sighed.

"But it's a start."

Milo looked up at him, something flickering behind his eyes.

Alden crossed his arms. "Every fight's about the same thing, kid—*control*. You can't control what they throw at you. You can't control what magic you've got. But you *can* control how you take a hit. How you keep standing. How you don't give them what they want."

Milo swallowed, nodding slowly.

"Alright. You're getting the stance. Now let's see how you move." He stepped back, rolling his shoulders. "If you're small, you use that. You don't let them keep you in one spot. You move."

Milo hesitated, shifting on his feet.

Alden tapped his knuckles against his palm. "Try dodging. Slow at first."

Milo furrowed his brow. "Like... sidestep?"

Alden smirked. "You tell me."

Milo took a deep breath and shifted to the left as Alden stepped toward him. It wasn't awful, but it wasn't good, either. His movement was slow, uncoordinated—he was thinking too much.

Alden reached out and lightly shoved his shoulder. Milo stumbled.

"Again," Alden said.

Milo reset.

Alden stepped forward, hands loose at his sides. This time, Milo moved faster, adjusting to the right before Alden could touch him. It wasn't clean, but it was better.

Alden nodded. "Good. But you're watching my hands. Don't."

Milo blinked. "What?"

Alden reached out and tapped the side of his boot with his own.

Milo flinched.

"Eyes on the shoulders and hips, not the hands," Alden said. "Hands lie. Shoulders don't."

Milo frowned, nodding again, adjusting his stance.

Alden stepped forward again. This time, the kid read the movement, shifting before Alden even got close.

Now that was real progress.

Alden crossed his arms. "At some point you're gonna get hit no matter what. Doesn't mean you have to make it easy for them."

Milo let out a breath. "I didn't fall that time."

Alden smirked. "Yeah. Try to keep it that way."

Milo straightened just a little, nodding again—this time with something actually resembling confidence.

Alden watched him for a moment, then exhaled through his nose. "One more thing."

Milo's confidence wavered. "Huh?"

"Fighting back isn't always the right move," Alden said. "Sometimes the best thing you can do is not be there when trouble starts."

Milo frowned. "You mean running?"

Alden shrugged. "Call it what you want. Running, retreating, choosing not to get your face kicked in—doesn't matter. The best fights are the ones you don't have to take." He tapped the kid's shoulder lightly. "You're small. Quick. Use that. Move before they can corner you. Hell, learn to spot trouble before it even starts."

Milo hesitated, considering that.

"Some fights you can't avoid," Alden continued. "When that happens, make sure you're still standing at the end of it. But if you can walk away before it starts? Even better."

Milo swallowed, then gave a single nod—less hesitant than before.

Alden jerked his head toward the stairs. "Now get to class before they think I'm recruiting child soldiers."

Milo let out a short laugh, shaking his head. "Right. Thanks."

He turned and hurried off.

Alden watched him go.

Poor kid. Hopefully that gives him an edge.

He exhaled, grabbed the brush, and went back to scrubbing.

CHAPTER
FIVE

The cafeteria buzzed with the usual midday energy—students talking, laughing, the clatter of trays against tables. The air carried the scent of roasted chicken and buttered rolls, a meal far more ordinary than what was coming later that night. Steak night.

Alden sat at the far end of the room, arms crossed, leaning back in his chair near the wall. Tobin Crane stood at his usual post, arms folded, surveying the room with his ever-watchful gaze.

Nothing seemed out of the ordinary.

Until Milo's tray hit the floor.

Alden didn't react. Just watched.

The cafeteria went quiet for a fraction of a second before students resumed their conversations. Some laughed under their breath. Others exchanged looks. Milo stood frozen at his table, staring at his now-empty spot. Across from him, a familiar smug grin stretched across the face of Darion Valcroft.

Alden sighed through his nose. *Should've known.*

Darion was one of those kids—the kind born into money, convinced that privilege made him untouchable. The Archduke's son, someone whose family name carried weight in places Alden didn't give a damn about.

Milo didn't say a word. He just turned and walked away.

Darion's grin widened.

Alden glanced toward Tobin. Tobin saw it. Did nothing.

That pissed him off more than anything else.

Milo didn't get far before Darion kicked out a foot.

Milo tripped, hitting the marble floor hard. A loud smack. A second of silence—then laughter rippled across the room.

Alden rolled his jaw. Still, he didn't move.

Tobin looked away.

That pissed Alden off even more.

Milo pushed himself up, blood dripping from his nose. He wiped at it with his sleeve, blinking away the sting. Darion chuckled, shaking his head. "You're pathetic, Ferin."

Milo didn't look at him. Just turned and kept walking.

Darion shoved him from behind.

Milo spun and threw a wild hook.

It barely grazed Darion's cheek, but the room still reacted. Gasps. Murmurs. A few shocked laughs.

Darion froze. His grin vanished. His eyes darkened.

Alden saw Tobin move, stepping forward, ready to break it up.

Alden lifted a hand.

Tobin stopped, turning to him with a raised brow.

Alden just shook his head.

Tobin hesitated, then stepped back. Alden turned his attention to the fight.

Darion's face twisted in a scowl. "You want to act tough now?" He lunged.

Milo dodged. Barely.

Alden saw it. The shift in his feet. The way he moved like he'd been paying attention.

Darion swung again. Milo stepped aside, just out of reach.

He wasn't fighting. He was avoiding. Defending. Just like Alden told him.

Darion swung harder and missed again, frustrating the young noble even more.

Milo was bleeding—nose, lip, maybe more—but he wasn't on the floor. That counted for a lot.

Alden allowed himself a small grin.

Darion growled, frustration mounting. He swung one last time, sloppy, angry, and Milo sidestepped it completely.

The room had gone quiet now.

Darion realized it too late. He huffed, straightening, trying to regain some dignity. He scoffed, brushing a hand over his cheek where Milo had clipped him.

"Not worth my time," Darion spat, turning away.

Alden's grin widened.

Darion caught it. His face turned red.

"This is your doing," he snarled, stepping toward Alden. Darion's scowl deepened. His hands curled into fists before he exhaled sharply and stormed off. "My father will hear about this."

Alden's smirk didn't fade. He'd heard worse threats.

Tobin didn't wait long before stepping up to him. "You know who that was, right?"

Alden picked at something on his sleeve. "Darion Valcroft."

"And do you know who his father is?"

Alden shrugged. "Archduke Somebody of Somewhere."

Tobin sighed. "Archduke Rendell Valcroft. Ruler of Vellmar."

Alden gave him a flat look. "Sounds important."

Tobin's lips pressed into a tight line. "The Archduke doesn't take slights lightly. You just embarrassed his son in front of half the academy."

"That's a shame." Alden shrugged. "Kid's gotta learn some manners sometime."

Tobin shook his head. "You don't care if you lose this job, do you?"

Alden smirked. "I was looking for a job when I found this one."

Tobin exhaled through his nose, rubbing his temples. "Unbelievable." He muttered something under his breath and walked off.

Alden leaned back in his chair, content. Until he saw something outside the windows.

His smirk faded.

Beyond the courtyard, just past the iron fence, something shifted. A shadow where there shouldn't be one. A flicker of movement. Too fast. Too precise.

Alden squinted.

Gone.

His gut twisted.

Before he could dwell on it, a voice pulled him back to reality.

"So, you taught little Milo how to fight, eh?"

Alden turned his head as Hugo Crevane approached, carrying a mug of some steaming liquid. The man had the presence of a general, despite the apron dusted with flour and the faint scent of spices that followed him wherever he went. His sharp, knowing eyes studied Alden like he was inspecting a fine cut of meat.

Alden shrugged. "Someone had to."

Hugo let out a low chuckle. "Not what I expected from you, Mr. Voss." He pulled out the chair opposite Alden and set the cup in front of him before sitting down. "You're full of surprises."

Alden glanced at the cup. "What's this?"

"Coffee." Hugo smirked. "Figured you could use it after babysitting all morning."

Alden grunted but took the cup anyway.

The cook leaned forward, resting his elbows on the table. "That was a fine lesson you gave the boy. Footwork was good. Hands were a little slow, but he'll get there."

Alden lifted a brow. "You watching the fights now, Crevane?"

Hugo shrugged. "I see more than you think. And I recognize a lesson passed down." He paused, studying Alden for a long moment. "You were a soldier."

Alden took a sip of coffee. "Lot of people were."

Hugo smirked. "Lot of people don't fight like that."

Alden didn't answer.

The cook leaned back, satisfied. "I'll have something special for you at supper tonight, Mr. Voss."

Alden tilted his head. "Weren't you already planning on cooking the steaks?"

Hugo chuckled. "Oh, the steak's for everyone. Your dish will be something a bit better."

Alden grunted. "Hope it's worth the trouble."

Hugo gave him a knowing look. "Trouble's already coming, my friend. I can feel it in the air." He stood and headed back toward the kitchen. "Time will tell."

Alden set the cup down, fingers tightening slightly.

You too, huh?

CHAPTER SIX

Alden left the cafeteria with Hugo's words still turning over in his mind.

Trouble's already coming, my friend. I can feel it in the air.

He shook off the unease.

The halls were quieter now. The usual midday chaos had settled a bit as students moved to their afternoon classes. The air had taken on a chill—subtle, but noticeable. A storm was coming. He could feel it in his bones.

Alden exhaled through his nose. That meant one more thing needed doing.

The enchanted boilers in the basement had to be restocked before the temperature dropped. Despite all the magic running through Warden's Rest, someone still had to load the firewood into the hoppers. The enchantments could handle the rest—heating water, running it through the pipes that snaked behind the walls—but the fuel itself had to be loaded by hand.

And that task, as always, fell to him. Which he was fine with. It was just another thing to keep his mind busy.

He made his way down the flight of stairs that led to the lower levels. The basement of Warden's Rest wasn't like the rest of the academy. The walls were thick and built from dark stone that seemed to swallow torchlight. The air carried the scent of damp earth and old machinery. Arcane boilers lined the far wall, glowing faintly from within. Each one was a towering beast of iron and brass with sigils etched into the plating.

When the fresh batch of firewood had been delivered earlier that week, he made sure to split it all and stack it neatly. All that was left was loading the hoppers and letting the machines do their work.

Alden grabbed an armful of wood and began feeding the massive boilers, letting the logs clatter into place. The enchantments hummed and gears shifted as magic flared. Within moments, the water in the pipes would be scalding hot, traveling through the academy's walls, pushing away the coming cold.

Alden dusted off his hands and rolled his shoulders.

One less thing to deal with.

By the time he made it back upstairs, the air felt heavier—that pre-storm weight pressing against the walls. The torches flickered as he made his way toward the janitorial closet, already thinking about the next mundane task of the day.

Something about the west wing windows—the seals needed checking before the rain rolled in.

Nothing difficult. Just another way to keep busy.

He was halfway there when a conversation caught his attention.

"...right across the face."

"No way."

"Swear on the gods. You should've seen Darion's face after—"

Alden slowed his steps, stopping just outside a corner where a handful of students stood gathered.

"It was wild," one of them said, leaning in toward the others. "Milo just... swung at him. No warning. Just cracked him across the cheek."

Alden felt the corners of his mouth twitch.

The first student grinned. "He dodged, too. Like, *really* dodged. Valcroft was swinging like an idiot, and he couldn't even land a hit."

The second student, a lanky girl with braided hair, scoffed. "Milo? No way."

"Swear it! Ask anyone who was in the cafeteria. Kid held his own. I mean, he got his face busted up, but still."

"Still," the girl echoed, shaking her head. "Didn't think he had it in him."

Alden smirked.

He stepped away from the conversation and continued down the hall, shaking his head.

Maybe the kid had more fight in him than I thought.

Alden kept walking as the conversation about Milo still lingered in his mind.

Fights had a way of turning into stories—sometimes bigger than they deserved to be. Some were exaggerated, others twisted into something unrecognizable, but this one had weight to it.

Milo had gone from punching bag to someone worth talking about. Just by standing up for himself.

That means something.

Alden reached the janitorial closet and pulled the door open. He rummaged through his neatly stacked supplies and grabbed a small satchel of tools for his next job. The west wing windows needed checking before the storm rolled in. Glass seals cracked over time, and if the rain got in, it wouldn't be his problem now—it'd be his problem later.

Better to handle it now than deal with students slipping in puddles for the next week.

He tossed the strap of the satchel over his shoulder and shut the closet. He rolled his shoulders and made his way toward the west wing.

The sky had darkened by the time he reached the outer halls. Thick, rolling clouds stretched across the horizon, swallowing what little sunlight remained. The storm was coming faster than expected.

He opened one of the tall glass windows, letting the evening air seep into the hall. Cool, crisp, with the faintest scent of rain.

He ran a hand along the window frame, feeling for cracks. Some of the older seals had weakened and the once-tight bindings had begun to warp with age. Nothing major—but enough to let in the cold if left unchecked.

Alden dug into his satchel, pulling out a small vial of sealant oil. The substance had a faint shimmer to it as it had been infused with minor enchantments meant to keep moisture out and structure intact.

Dip the brush. Apply to the frame. Let the magic set.

Simple.

The kind of work he actually liked—quiet, useful—didn't involve breaking bones or faces.

He moved to the next window, repeating the process. Out in the courtyard, the wind picked up, rustling the trees beyond the fence.

Alden was halfway through the last window when the feeling returned.

That sensation of being watched.

Slow. Creeping. Like something was just out of sight.

He didn't move right away.

Didn't look up.

Instead, he focused on his breathing, keeping it steady and measured. His fingers tightened around the brush, but otherwise, he acted as if nothing was wrong.

He finished sealing the frame and casually glanced outside.

Something was there. A figure, just past the fence. A shadow against the trees. The wind blew, bending the branches, shifting the light. For a moment, Alden could swear he saw a shape standing there.

Then, it was gone.

His gut twisted.

The rational part of his mind wanted to dismiss it. A trick of the light. A moving shadow. A cloud passing over the last shreds of daylight.

But his instincts?

They never lied.

Something was out there.

Waiting.

Watching.

Alden exhaled slowly and closed the window.

The storm wasn't the only thing rolling in.

CHAPTER SEVEN

Alden stood motionless by the window for another moment, eyes fixed on the spot where he'd seen the shadow. The wind grew sharper, rattling the panes softly, tugging at branches as it whispered promises of the storm soon to arrive. But whatever had been out there, whatever had watched from the shadows, was gone.

He shook his head slightly, irritation settling into his bones. He had responsibilities—mundane tasks to do. Tasks that no one else would remember or even notice unless they were left undone.

He packed away the small vial of sealant and the brush, rolling his shoulders to loosen the growing stiffness. The sun was setting faster than he'd expected, painting the sky in hues of bruised purple and angry red. With the approaching darkness, the academy's lamps and enchanted sconces flickered to life, casting warm, golden pools of light against the deepening gloom of the halls.

Alden closed the window, setting the latch. It clicked softly into place. For a moment he just stood there, fingers lingering on the cool brass, his thoughts tangled around the shifting shadow he'd seen at the fence line.

He shook his head and stepped back. No use getting paranoid—not yet. Even if his gut was rarely wrong, he needed something more substantial than a vague feeling and a flicker of shadow.

But he'd learned long ago not to dismiss instinct entirely.

He turned away from the window, and headed toward the faculty offices. If anyone else had noticed something strange, they'd be there. Maybe he wasn't the only one with uneasy thoughts.

The halls felt colder now, as if the storm outside was seeping through the very stone of the building. A distant rumble of thunder growled, resonating through the corridors like a warning. Students hurried past, quiet, subdued, likely sensing the same subtle shift in the air.

He found Orin Hale first, standing in front of his office, arms folded, eyes fixed on one of the large decorative windows that overlooked the main courtyard.

Orin glanced his way as he approached. "Alden."

"Orin," Alden replied, nodding toward the window. "You saw something too?"

Orin's jaw tightened slightly, an admission without words. "I see shadows where there shouldn't be any. Been like that most of the afternoon." His voice dropped lower. "I thought I was imagining things."

"You weren't." Alden paused, following Orin's gaze. "Someone's watching the academy. Saw a figure myself. It didn't stick around long enough to be sure of anything else."

Orin exhaled, the tension visibly deepening in his posture. "I don't like this. The Dean's explanations earlier... none of this sits right. We should've been given more to go on."

Alden shrugged. "Someone higher up doesn't trust us enough with the details of wherever the senior staff ran off to."

"Or," Orin said quietly, his tone darkening, "they don't want us involved."

Alden frowned. That had been exactly his thought. "Doesn't matter now, though, does it?"

Orin sighed, shaking his head. "No, I suppose it doesn't."

"Where's Tobin?" Alden asked.

"In the training hall, sharpening swords like it's going out of style," Orin answered. "Says it helps him think."

Alden grunted. "I'll see if he's seen anything else."

Orin nodded once, turning back to the window, eyes narrowed in quiet suspicion. "If you see Milena or Evora, tell them to keep an eye out. I'll reinforce the wards. Quietly, just in case."

"Good," Alden said. "We might need it."

The cavernous training hall, lined with racks of enchanted weapons, scorched training dummies, and battered shields, sat at the far end of the faculty wing. Tobin stood at a whetstone, slowly drawing the blade of a longsword across it in careful, practiced movements.

He glanced up as Alden entered, pausing only briefly before continuing the motion. "Need something?"

"Orin says you're overthinking things," Alden said dryly, leaning against one of the racks. "Figured I'd see for myself."

Tobin snorted. "If Orin paid attention half as much as he worries, the wards wouldn't need reinforcing every few weeks."

Alden gave a faint grin. "You noticed that too, did you?"

Tobin stopped sharpening and placed the sword carefully on the table. His gaze turned serious. "How couldn't I? You were right. Warden's Rest feels exposed. Vulnerable, even, without the senior staff."

"Orin's already reinforcing the wards, quietly." Alden crossed his arms, considering. "But something tells me wards might not be enough this time."

Tobin raised an eyebrow. "Got something more specific, or just that old centurion gut acting up?"

"Both," Alden admitted, shrugging slightly. "Saw someone lurking near the gates. Watching us. Watching the academy."

"Someone?" Tobin's eyes narrowed sharply. "As in just one?"

Alden shook his head slowly. "One that I saw. Maybe more. Couldn't get a clear look."

Tobin's hand drifted toward the sword hilt resting nearby. "Sounds like scouting. Tactical positioning, if I had to guess."

"Exactly," Alden agreed. "And with the senior staff conveniently off-campus…"

"Just a tad *too* convenient," Tobin finished. "Someone knows exactly what they're doing."

Alden nodded, feeling his own suspicion deepen. "Which means we need to be ready. No senior staff means the students are defenseless if something happens."

Tobin exhaled sharply. "We've got a handful of teachers, a legendary chef, and an old soldier with a mop. Not exactly what I'd call battle-ready."

Alden felt the corner of his mouth twitch. "I've seen worse odds."

Tobin managed a faint smirk. "I suppose you have."

They fell into a momentary silence, broken only by the low, distant rumble of thunder echoing through the academy. Alden glanced toward the training hall doors, thoughts drifting briefly toward the rest of the staff—Milena's elemental fury, Evora's shadow games, Orin's wards. They were capable, certainly, but coordinated defense required more than individual skill.

"You should talk to Evora," Tobin said suddenly, interrupting his thoughts. "She's sharp—sees things others miss. If we're missing a bigger picture here, she might have already pieced it together."

Alden pushed off from the weapon rack, nodding once. "I'll find her."

As Alden reached the door, Tobin's voice stopped him again, softer this time. "Keep your guard up, Alden. Something tells me we're going to need more than wards and steel to handle whatever's coming."

Alden paused, glancing back. "Already planned on it."

The halls were emptier now as Alden headed toward Evora's study. Evening classes had begun, and the silence seemed heavier—

like the academy itself was holding its breath. He found Evora's door slightly ajar, shadows flickering strangely at its edges.

He knocked once and pushed the door open slowly. "Evora?"

Evora Nightvale stood near her desk, hands extended, tendrils of shadow twining around her fingers as if they were alive. She turned slowly, her eyes dark pools that reflected the dim room behind her.

"I was wondering when you'd find me," she said softly, shadows fading from her fingertips. "You've seen them too, haven't you?"

"Yeah," Alden said, stepping inside and closing the door behind him. "Thought it was just me at first. But Orin and Tobin have either seen or felt it as well."

Evora's eyes flicked toward the window, thoughtful. "There's magic out there, Alden. Hidden. Powerful. Watching."

He crossed his arms, the knot of tension tightening further. "Any idea who or why?"

Her expression was grim, the shadows in the room lengthening as she spoke. "No, but they're waiting for something. A signal, maybe. Or just the right moment."

"Waiting," Alden echoed, his gut tightening. He shook his head. "I need to finish up for the day. Going to hit the library and then head to the cafeteria."

Evora smirked at him. "A bit of light reading? You?"

Alden scoffed. "I read books," he said as he turned to leave. "Sometimes."

Evora chuckled behind him.

CHAPTER
EIGHT

The day's last chore was already nagging at him from the back of his mind. It wasn't exciting or glamorous, but it was important. Alden sighed and turned toward the main corridor. His boots echoed softly against the polished stone floors as he made his way toward the school's grand library.

Few students were inside this late, most already preparing for supper or finishing homework elsewhere. But the library wasn't merely a place to study—it was a repository for ancient knowledge and arcane texts. Enchantments and preservation spells carefully maintained each volume. Still, dust accumulated, and shifting weather caused moisture that could damage delicate pages if left unchecked.

Alden entered quietly, giving a polite nod to the librarian, a kindly older woman named Elysia, who spent most of her days gently scolding students who mishandled books. She glanced up from her desk, smiling warmly.

Her silver hair was coiled into a tight bun, a pair of delicate half-moon spectacles perched on the bridge of her nose. Dozens of ink smudges stained her fingertips, and she draped a deep burgundy shawl, embroidered with little stitched runes, over her shoulders like a second skin. Her presence radiated quiet authority—the kind that made even the rowdiest students whisper when they stepped foot into her domain.

"Evening, Alden," she greeted softly.

"Elysia," he replied with a slight tilt of his head. "Everything alright today?"

"Oh, the usual. Half the students wouldn't recognize proper respect for a tome if it bit them in the tush," she said with mild amusement. Her smile faltered slightly as her eyes took on a thoughtful expression. "Though the air feels odd today. Thicker, somehow."

Alden hummed quietly. "Storm's coming. Maybe that's it?"

Elysia considered this, nodding slowly. "Perhaps. Well, do your best with the shelves. And be gentle, will you?"

"Always," Alden assured her, gathering a handful of soft cloths from a cabinet behind her desk. "I'll be careful."

The shelves stretched upward nearly two stories, spiraling toward a ceiling enchanted to mirror the night sky outside, stars twinkling faintly as if through a veil of clouds. Alden began his task methodically, wiping down the wooden shelves gently, dusting leather-bound tomes that hummed faintly with latent magic. It was tedious work, but he found a certain peace in its repetition.

As he moved along the upper rows, he couldn't help but glance down at the titles. The Artifice of Protection. Defensive Sigils and Their Uses. Principles of Arcane Fortification. He smirked to himself. Books he'd never read, but whose contents he'd experienced first-hand, etched into his memory through long, hard years.

He paused for a moment, fingers lingering over the gilded spine of an old, worn text titled The Battle of Eldermoor. It had been required reading for generations of spellblades and centurions—tactical lessons embedded between pages recounting bravery and bloodshed. Alden sighed, shaking his head to clear away unwanted memories, and continued down the row.

The quiet scrape of wood against stone drew his attention downward. At the far end of the library, Milo Ferin sat hunched over a small table, oblivious to Alden's presence. The boy's bruises had darkened further, deep purple shadows beneath the flickering lamplight. Alden's gut twisted slightly.

He descended slowly, keeping his steps deliberately loud enough to announce himself. Milo startled at the sound, jerking upright and turning wide, anxious eyes toward him.

"Oh," Milo said, relaxing slightly as he recognized Alden. "It's you."

"Who else would it be?" Alden responded, returning to his work but keeping the boy within view. "You alright?"

"Yeah," Milo mumbled, clearly lying.

Alden grunted softly. "You don't have to pretend around me, kid."

Milo hesitated, fiddling with the corner of his book. "I guess not."

The silence stretched comfortably for a moment before Milo spoke again, voice quiet and uncertain. "Do you think I'll ever get stronger?"

Alden paused, contemplating his answer. "Strength isn't always about size or magic, Milo. Sometimes it's just about endurance. Getting up again when everything tells you to stay down."

Milo nodded slowly. "Does it get easier?"

Alden chuckled darkly. "No. But you get tougher."

Milo sighed, seeming to weigh the words carefully. "Thanks."

Alden inclined his head briefly, resuming his cleaning. After several minutes, Milo gathered his belongings and stood to leave, offering a quiet goodnight as he slipped out into the hallway.

Alden watched him go, thoughtful. He turned back toward the shelves, hesitated, then called softly, "Hold on a second, Milo."

The boy paused in the doorway, turning around with cautious curiosity.

Alden pulled two slim volumes from a nearby shelf and

approached, holding them out to the boy. "Go ask the librarian to check these out for you."

Milo accepted them uncertainly, glancing down at the titles. "The Tempest Chronicles... and The Aetheric Codex?" He looked up, brow furrowed. "What are these?"

"Consider it required reading," Alden replied. He tapped the cover of the first book. "The Tempest Chronicles—it's about ordinary folks caught in extraordinary times, people who chose to fight back when nobody else would." He nodded toward the second. "And The Aetheric Codex is about power, responsibility, and what it really means to wield magic. Read them. Might give you some perspective."

Milo's fingers tightened around the books. He swallowed, then met Alden's gaze. "You think I'll understand them?"

"You already do." Alden placed a firm hand on Milo's shoulder. "You just don't know it yet. When you're done with those, ask the librarian for a copy of The Battle of Eldermoor."

Milo straightened, holding the books close. He nodded once, resolute. "Thank you, Mr. Voss."

Alden gave a gentle push toward the hallway. "Now get some rest. Tomorrow's another long day."

Milo smiled faintly and left the library, a little taller than when he'd entered.

Alden watched him go, then turned back to the endless rows of bookshelves, quietly resuming his duties.

Alden finished his work in silence, placing the cleaning cloths back into the cabinet and giving a respectful nod to Elysia as he exited the library. She smiled softly, offering him a weary wave in return.

The halls outside had grown dark, illuminated only by the faint, magical glow of sconces set into the stone walls. Alden paused, glancing down the length of the corridor toward the front gates, still uneasy.

His stomach tightened again as the feeling returned, stronger this time.

Waiting. Watching.

He shook himself sharply, irritation mingling with unease. No matter what was out there, the academy had defenses, wards, enchantments, skilled teachers—this wasn't some unprotected village. He clenched his fists, turning deliberately toward the staff quarters. Supper was approaching, and Hugo's Void-Crusted Steak awaited him.

Whatever waited beyond the gates, whatever darkness threatened to encroach upon this sanctuary, it would have to wait its turn. Alden Voss had other problems to face first.

Like an empty stomach and a cook who brooked no tardiness at his table.

CHAPTER NINE

The sky had darkened further and the clouds now stretched across the horizon like ink spilling across parchment. Thunder rolled quietly in the distance, promising a storm whose approach felt far too well-timed. Alden was making his way back from Evora's study with her ominous warnings still fresh in his thoughts.

Whatever was happening, it wasn't random. They weren't dealing with isolated coincidences or the misplaced paranoia of a few tired faculty members. It was planned, deliberate, and rapidly approaching.

He passed by several classrooms, peering through half-open doors at the oblivious students scribbling notes or listening to lectures on magical theory and arcane defense—lessons he suspected would soon become far too practical. Each hallway he crossed felt emptier than the last, as if the academy itself was bracing for impact.

Alden turned the corner into the long, window-lined corridor leading toward the front of the academy. He halted abruptly, eyes narrowing at the figures standing silently outside the massive wrought-iron gates.

There were at least half a dozen of them, perhaps more, all wrapped in dark traveling cloaks with deep hoods drawn low over their faces. They didn't appear to carry weapons openly, but Alden recognized the posture of warriors immediately—feet planted at measured distances, hands ready at their sides. A faint glimmer caught his eye as one of the cloaked figures shifted—a blade briefly revealed at the waist before vanishing back into shadow.

They definitely weren't students, nor were they visiting faculty. Every instinct Alden possessed screamed that these people were dangerous, disciplined, and lethal.

He exhaled slowly. "Fantastic."

He stepped cautiously forward, minimizing his movement as he edged closer to one of the tall windows and peered carefully through the glass, trying to gauge their intent. They demonstrated organization, calmness, and patience. That was the most unsettling part. They weren't here by accident or on a whim—they were waiting.

As he watched, another shadow shifted just beyond the edge of the gates, something far larger than the cloaked figures. His chest tightened. He'd seen enough battles to recognize the hulking outline immediately, even at this distance.

"Bloody hell," he whispered under his breath, heart sinking. "A damned war troll."

The hulking silhouette moved briefly into clearer view before sinking back into the darkness of the treeline. War trolls weren't subtle weapons—they were siege-breakers, destructive forces wielded by those who meant to shatter defenses utterly and swiftly.

Alden turned on his heel, urgency burning in his veins. They had to prepare immediately. Warden's Rest Academy was strong. Layers of arcane wards and powerful enchantments fortified it, but no defense was invincible—especially not when the defenders were a handful of junior faculty members and a janitor with nothing but a mop and a bad attitude.

He strode quickly toward Tobin's office, not bothering with courtesy as he pushed the door open without knocking. Tobin sat at his desk, scribbling notes onto a piece of parchment, the pen freezing mid-stroke as he glanced up, startled.

"Alden? Is everything—"

"We've got trouble," Alden interrupted, shutting the door firmly behind him. "*Real* trouble."

Tobin dropped the pen, standing quickly. "What did you see?"

"Group of armed figures at the front gates," Alden said, voice grim. "Mercenaries. Spellblades, by the looks of them. And they brought a war troll."

"A war troll?" Tobin repeated, disbelief quickly replaced by something more pragmatic. "You're sure?"

"Never been more certain," Alden replied. "I've fought alongside and against enough of them to recognize their shape. It's waiting at the treeline. Probably meant to breach the gates when the attack starts."

Tobin cursed softly, rubbing his forehead. "And with half our staff missing... gods, we're vulnerable."

"Exactly." Alden folded his arms, his posture stiffening as adrenaline surged through him. "We need to alert the others right away. Orin's wards might buy us a little time, but wards alone won't stop a troll and mercenaries who came prepared."

Tobin nodded sharply, grabbing a heavy cloak and a sword from a hook near his door. "Let's move. The sooner we organize the others, the better chance we have of protecting the students."

Together, they strode from the office and down the empty hallway. The academy felt unnaturally quiet now. The students were unaware of the imminent danger gathering just beyond their walls. Alden had seen enough battles to know the eerie quiet that always came before chaos.

They found Orin in the main atrium, inspecting one of the large decorative statues carved from enchanted marble. He straightened as Alden and Tobin approached, immediately sensing the urgency in their steps.

"What is it?" Orin asked cautiously.

"Mercenaries at the gates," Tobin answered quickly. "At least half a dozen, probably more—and Alden spotted a war troll lurking nearby."

Orin paled, mouth tightening into a thin line. "A war troll? Damn it all. We need to move quickly—I'll reinforce the primary wards. Evora should be in the cafeteria helping Hugo prepare the evening meal."

Alden nodded once. "We'll head there immediately."

Orin frowned. "Ask if Hugo has anything stored in that kitchen that could double as weaponry or magical enhancements. Now would be the time to use it."

Tobin exhaled slowly. "We'll gather the students once the wards are secure. Best case, this blows over without incident. Worst case—"

"Worst case," Alden interrupted firmly, "we're fighting to keep them alive."

Orin didn't reply immediately, his eyes briefly closed in quiet calculation. When he opened them again, his voice was firm and decisive. "Do what you must. I'll build up the wards and buy us as much time as possible." He moved swiftly toward the main staircase, chanting softly beneath his breath as a shimmering barrier of protective wards flickered faintly into existence around him. "Don't wait for me. I'll meet you in the cafeteria."

Alden and Tobin exchanged a tense glance before hurrying toward the cafeteria. The calm still held within the school, but Alden could feel it fraying at the edges—every breath, every echoing footstep felt like a countdown to violence.

As they walked, Tobin glanced toward Alden. The tightness in his jaw betrayed his apprehension. "You really didn't sign up for this, did you?"

Alden grunted softly, grim determination settling into his chest. "Did any of us?" He shrugged. "War never really leaves us alone."

Tobin grimaced, but said nothing else.

Alden shoved the cafeteria doors open. Evora and Hugo were deep in quiet conversation. Evora's expression was tense. Hugo's brows knitted together in concern.

"What is it?" she asked.

"Trouble," grumbled Hugo. "I'd recognize the sight of someone mentally preparing themselves for battle anywhere."

Alden stepped into the room and nodded. "Mercenaries and a war troll at the gates. We don't have long."

Hugo straightened slowly with an old, dangerous gleam in his eyes. "Then it's fortunate I didn't use all my tricks in the last war."

Alden managed a humorless smile. "Good. Because we'll need every trick we can get."

CHAPTER TEN

A deep, resonant boom shattered the quiet, shaking the academy, rattling windows, and sending vibrations through the stone floors. Alden steadied himself against the cafeteria doorframe, heart hammering as instinct took over.

Tobin shot him a hard look. "They're already inside?"

"Not yet," Alden growled, glancing through the tall, ornate windows lining the cafeteria walls. "That blast was at the front gates."

From the distant hallway, Evora's voice suddenly echoed, calm yet authoritative, magically amplified by the academy's emergency ward system.

"All students, report to the cafeteria immediately. Remain calm and orderly. This is not a drill. Repeat, all students to the cafeteria immediately."

Tobin's jaw tightened as murmurs and hurried footsteps began filling the halls. The growing cacophony punctuated by sharp, anxious whispers. Within moments, students poured into the cafeteria from every adjoining corridor, confusion and concern plain on their young faces.

Evora emerged moments later, moving quickly toward Alden and Tobin. Her dark robes billowed slightly around her ankles as shadows trailed behind her like liquid smoke.

"The wards at the front gate failed completely," she said, voice tense but composed. "Orin managed to bolster the secondary barriers, but they won't hold long against this kind of assault."

"Did you see what caused that blast?" Alden asked grimly.

She nodded once, eyes narrowed. "Fire magic—highly concentrated. Whoever these mercenaries are, they've brought powerful spellblades. The gate is gone. Completely obliterated."

Tobin cursed under his breath. "I was afraid of that. These attackers aren't just random bandits or opportunists. They're professionals."

"We need to organize the defense," Evora said. "With the senior faculty away, it's up to us to keep the students safe."

Alden glanced toward Hugo, who stood calmly behind the cafeteria's serving counter, quickly organizing several large sacks of enchanted spices and oils—ingredients Alden suspected were far more volatile and likely less legal than anything a normal kitchen would contain.

"You seem ready," Alden remarked dryly.

Hugo's eyes flicked up, a quiet confidence glinting beneath the outward calm. "War never really leaves you, does it, Mr. Voss?"

"No," Alden admitted. "It certainly doesn't."

More impacts echoed throughout the academy. Each successive blast drew nearer, accompanied by the unmistakable sound of shattering glass and fracturing stone. Alden's gut tightened further with each tremor. He knew those sounds all too well: siege tactics meant to break morale and structure alike.

He turned quickly, facing Evora and Tobin. "We're running out of time. We need positions. Tobin, you're our strongest frontline—hold the main corridor near the entrance. Evora, stay here in the cafeteria. Your shadow veil can shield the students and buy us some time. Hugo—"

Hugo raised an eyebrow, clearly amused despite the seriousness of the situation. "The cafeteria will not fall."

Alden nodded sharply. "Good. I'll find Orin and try to reinforce whatever wards we have left."

Tobin straightened as steel resolve settled into his eyes. "Understood. We'll hold as long as possible."

As Tobin departed, barking quick orders to the older students to help barricade doors, Alden moved toward the cafeteria exit. Evora's shadows deepened around her. She traced faint sigils in the air with her fingers as protective barriers wove into existence, partially obscuring the entrance with a shifting veil of darkness.

Another blast shook the walls, this one dangerously close, and Alden broke into a run. The corridor ahead was filling rapidly with panicked students still making their way toward the cafeteria. He shouted instructions, directing them urgently as he pushed forward, his boots pounding on stone.

When he finally reached Orin, he found the professor kneeling near the central atrium, hands pressed to the marble floor, eyes closed tight. Sweat beaded on his forehead as glowing sigils spread outward from his fingertips, forming a flickering lattice across the floor and walls.

Alden skidded to a halt beside him. "Orin, can you hold it?"

Orin didn't answer immediately, his breath ragged as his concentration strained. Finally, he gasped, opening his eyes. "Not for long. They're tearing through my wards faster than I can rebuild them."

Alden glanced toward the towering windows at the far end of the atrium. Dread pooled in his stomach. Dark figures approached in disciplined formation. They crossed the ruined courtyard beyond the shattered gates and stepped carefully over twisted remnants of molten iron and cracked stone pillars.

At the rear of the formation, a monstrous shadow lumbered forward, enormous shoulders rolling beneath armored plates, massive fists clenched at its sides. Alden's pulse quickened as recognition sank in: the war troll, now fully visible, loomed like a siege engine amid the mercenary ranks.

Orin followed his gaze and swore under his breath. "Gods preserve us."

"Save your prayers," Alden growled, grabbing Orin's shoulder and hauling him upright. "Can you reinforce just the interior doors in order to funnel them into the main corridor?"

Orin nodded weakly. "Yes, but it'll take almost everything I have left."

"Do it," Alden said sharply. "We have to slow them down. Tobin's already there."

Another explosion echoed. The academy shuddered beneath the assault. A plume of flame erupted from a side corridor. Students scattered in terror. Alden's chest tightened further—*we need to hurry.*

Orin steadied himself as he channeled energy into one last, desperate incantation. The sigils on the floor flared brightly before fading to a dull, steady glow.

"Done," he breathed, sagging against Alden for support. "The main corridor is now their only route inside. I sealed everything else—for now."

Alden set him carefully against a nearby wall. "Stay here. Recover as quickly as you can. Do you have any mana potions?"

"In my office," he whispered.

Alden nodded. "Lock yourself in your office, use the potions, and keep those wards up as long as you can."

Orin nodded. "Good luck, Alden."

As Alden rushed back toward the main corridor, Evora's voice echoed once more, still controlled, but now edged with urgency.

"All remaining students, get to the cafeteria immediately. Staff members, hold your positions."

The academy's magical torches sputtered as the mercenaries drew nearer. Alden rounded the corner, joining Tobin at the corridor entrance.

Alden looked through the shattered glass and gaping holes in the stone walls. Cloaked figures advanced steadily, blades drawn and spell energy crackling between outstretched hands.

At their center, the war troll moved slowly and deliberately. Lingering flames from the gates it had breached illuminated its enormous armored bulk.

Tobin adjusted his stance, sword raised, face pale but resolute. "If we survive this, remind me to take retirement more seriously."

Alden exhaled slowly. "One step at a time, Tobin. Let's survive first."

Outside, the mercenaries charged forward, spells igniting the air. The war troll roared, a sound of pure primal fury that resonated deep within Alden's bones.

The siege had begun in earnest.

CHAPTER
ELEVEN

A surge of fire blasted through the corridor, scorching the stone walls and forcing Alden and Tobin into a hasty retreat. Tobin threw up a shimmering barrier with a shouted incantation, deflecting the worst of the flames, but Alden still felt their oppressive heat searing the air inches from his face.

He didn't hesitate. Years of battle experience took over—a familiar rhythm he hadn't felt in far too long guided his actions. "Fall back!" he shouted. "Slowly—stay together!"

Tobin grunted in acknowledgment, maintaining the magical barrier as they retreated step by deliberate step, their eyes fixed firmly ahead on the advancing mercenaries. These attackers moved with unsettling precision, their movements synchronized, disciplined. They unleashed volley after volley of elemental spells—flame, lightning, and jagged shards of ice that splintered against Tobin's shield with resounding cracks.

Behind the frontline, Alden glimpsed the war troll steadily advancing, massive feet crushing debris beneath its weight, its enormous fists methodically battering aside the remnants of doors and barricades. Its scarred and calloused hide was armored in overlapping plates that faintly shimmered. Wards etched into the metal amplified its natural resistance. They'd come prepared. These were no common raiders, but mercenaries equipped to shatter defenses far more formidable than a single magical academy.

"Tobin," Alden called sharply, catching the combat instructor's attention. "We're losing ground. We need a chokepoint."

Tobin exhaled sharply as sweat ran down his brow from the strain of maintaining his barrier. "Cafeteria entrance—narrow doors, reinforced walls. It's our best shot."

Alden nodded. "Then move. I'll cover you."

Tobin hesitated only briefly, concern clear in his gaze. "You sure?"

"Go," Alden insisted, voice iron-hard. "If your barrier breaks before we reach the cafeteria, none of this will matter."

Tobin's jaw tightened, but he obeyed, stepping back quickly. He let the shield ripple as Alden stepped forward to take his place. Alden's own magic surged forward—protective, fortifying—strengthening the very air around him until it felt solid; almost tangible.

A relentless torrent of flame erupted again. It cascaded toward Alden. He raised an arm reflexively, feeling the wave of heat wash over him, his own magic absorbing most of the energy. It was a temporary defense, but it bought precious seconds as he continued to back slowly toward the cafeteria doors, watching closely as Tobin moved quickly to prepare their next line of defense.

The mercenaries pressed forward steadily, testing Alden's magical defenses with precise, measured strikes. The force of their spells threw their hoods back, revealing their faces. Their faces showed focus and calm—no fear, no hesitation. These men and women had done this before, countless times. To them, Warden's Rest was merely another objective; another payday.

Frustration and anger boiled beneath Alden's carefully maintained composure. This was his home now, and these students, despite their quirks and antics, were under his protection. He'd be damned if he'd allow mercenary scum to stroll through these halls uncontested.

A second volley surged forward—this time a bolt of crackling lightning arced toward Alden, striking him with a deafening clap. He staggered under the impact. His vision momentarily darkened, but he held firm. Tobin called urgently from behind him, "Alden! It's ready—fall back!"

He turned swiftly, sprinting the last short distance to the cafeteria entrance, where Tobin and Evora had already begun reinforcing the doors. Evora's shadow magic had coalesced into a dense, living barrier—its tendrils coiled protectively around the heavy wooden doors, strengthening them with layers of shifting darkness.

Alden slid through just as Tobin slammed the door shut behind him. Evora's shadows enveloped it fully. He leaned heavily against the wall, breathing sharply.

"Where's Orin?" he asked.

"Locked in his office," said Alden between breaths. "Had some mana potions stashed in there, so he's reinforcing the wards as best he can." He looked around. "And Milena?"

"Already inside," said Evora as shadows receded slightly from around her hands. "She's gathering a small group of advanced students to bolster the defense."

Alden nodded, regaining his breath. Around them, wide-eyed students clustered nervously. Their faces were pale and their voices hushed. Tangible and potent fear radiated from them, filling the air with tension. It was only natural, Alden knew—but it was also dangerous. Fear could lead to panic, and panic would break their fragile defenses faster than any mercenary spellblade.

He straightened, projecting a calm he didn't entirely feel. "Listen carefully," he said, voice steady, loud enough to reach the gathered students. "The academy is under attack. We're holding here—this room is our stronghold. Stay calm, and do exactly as the teachers tell you. We'll get through this."

A voice piped up nervously, trembling slightly. "Who are they?"

Alden shook his head slightly. "Mercenaries—professional attackers. They're organized, well-trained. But they're not invincible. We just have to hold and wear them down."

Another student, a tall boy with determination etched onto his features, stepped forward. "What can we do?"

Tobin glanced at Alden, uncertain. Alden looked directly at the boy, considering him carefully. He recognized him—Tristan, a senior. Responsible. Solid under pressure.

"Help barricade the back entrances," Alden said decisively. "Secure any secondary access points. Tobin and Evora need to focus their magic forward. We'll trust you to watch our backs."

Tristan nodded, already moving with a small group toward the rear of the cafeteria.

"Good," Alden muttered softly, more to himself than anyone else. Initiative would keep their minds busy and fear at bay.

The heavy cafeteria doors shuddered under sudden impact. Magic sparked against Evora's shadow wards, reminding Alden that time was short. Evora grunted softly, bracing herself, but her barriers held strong.

Hugo appeared suddenly at Alden's side, carrying an assortment of sealed bottles and sacks filled with powder. "Alden, take these. Enchanted spices and oil. They ignite fiercely under the right conditions."

Alden accepted the improvised weapons gratefully. "You're full of surprises, Crevane."

The cook's smile was grim. "These halls were peaceful, but I've learned long ago to prepare for war."

Alden moved quickly, distributing Hugo's weapons to Tobin and several older students who had limited combat training. The cafeteria grew quieter as tension pressed upon them like a physical weight as the attackers outside prepared their next move.

Alden stepped forward, placing himself firmly at the center of their defenses. The doors shook violently. Splinters flew from the reinforced wood as it cracked under relentless assault.

"Hold firm!" Alden called, rallying everyone within earshot. "We protect the academy. We protect each other."

His voice resonated, firm and unyielding, echoing his determination.

Then, with an ear-splitting crack, chunks of the doors shattered inward.

CHAPTER TWELVE

Splinters of wood sprayed inward as the doors buckled, held together only by the lingering strength of Evora's magic. Alden felt his pulse pounding in his temples, but adrenaline sharpened his focus to a razor's edge. The students closest to him instinctively drew back, but Alden stepped forward, his presence solidifying like a stone wall between them and the threat beyond.

"Stay calm," Alden said firmly, raising his voice just enough to carry authority without panic. "We're ready for them."

He turned quickly, scanning the room until his eyes met Tristan's. The senior stood by the rear barricade. His face was steady and resolved, despite the chaos erupting around them.

"Tristan!" Alden called sharply. "Get your group ready. You're our secondary line. If those doors fall completely, hold that choke point. Understood?"

Tristan nodded immediately, already turning to the surrounding students, giving swift orders with a confidence that belied his age. Alden felt a surge of pride, brief but powerful—there was hope yet, even in chaos.

Evora stood with arms outstretched. Shadows twisted and

writhed at her fingertips as she strained to reinforce what was left of the barricade. Tobin moved beside her, chanting incantations quietly under his breath, weaving layers of protective spells atop her dark veil. Their combined magic shimmered and pulsed visibly. It was a formidable barrier, yet Alden knew even that wouldn't hold forever.

"Hugo," Alden shouted, turning swiftly toward the kitchen area. The cook looked up sharply, hands deftly sorting through his supply of enchanted spices and improvised explosive materials. "You and Milena—prepare your strongest defensive enchantments and keep them ready. If they breach, we'll need immediate containment."

Hugo inclined his head sharply. "Consider it done, Mr. Voss."

Alden stepped forward again, standing close behind Evora and Tobin, bolstering their resolve with his own steady presence. He glanced quickly around the cafeteria, assessing their situation once more, noting the faces of the students clustered together, frightened but steady. Many had armed themselves with whatever was nearby —chairs, table legs, utensils sharpened hastily with basic spells. It was crude, improvised, but it was determination in physical form, and it mattered.

A voice sounded urgently from the side, and Alden turned to see Milena quickly approaching, breathing hard. "All students are accounted for. Every last one of them."

Alden nodded sharply. "Good work."

She gave a tight smile, determined but strained. "We're ready to follow your lead, Alden."

Alden blinked, briefly taken aback by the simple honesty in her voice, then straightened, feeling the weight of their trust settle onto his shoulders with a familiar heaviness. "We hold together, Milena. Just keep everyone steady."

The next blow against the barricade was stronger than before. Alden felt it vibrate through the stone floor beneath him. Evora staggered slightly, gasping as the shadow barrier flickered dangerously.

"It won't hold much longer," Evora warned, her voice shaking slightly from strain. Tobin steadied her with one hand on her shoulder, eyes locked ahead.

Then, with a deafening crash, the barricade splintered more. Chunks of wood scattered across the floor. The barrier held, barely, but left a gaping hole in its center—large enough to see clearly through to the invaders standing just beyond.

Outside, arranged in disciplined ranks, stood the mercenary force. Their dark cloaks were cast back now, revealing the hardened faces beneath their polished helmets. Arcane runes glowed faintly on their armor and weapons, signaling preparations for another wave of magical assault.

But their attack didn't resume immediately. Instead, from behind their lines came a single commanding voice, amplified by magic and echoing clearly through the ruined barricade.

"Hold fire!"

The voice reverberated powerfully. It was filled with a calm authority that demanded attention. The mercenaries halted instantly and lowered their weapons, though they remained alert and poised to strike again at a word.

A figure stepped forward. He was taller and more confident than the rest, carrying himself with unmistakable command. The man strode calmly toward the shattered entrance, stopping just outside the reach of Evora's shadow magic. His dark cloak rippled slightly in the breeze. The faint glow of lingering enchantments illuminated clearly his sharp features.

The man's eyes swept slowly across the gathered defenders inside, assessing and calculating. Alden recognized that look—it was the look of someone accustomed to command. One who rarely encountered meaningful resistance.

"I wish to speak to whoever is in charge," he announced coolly, his amplified voice carrying easily across the room, filling every tense, breathless silence that followed. "There's no need for further bloodshed."

Silence hung thickly in the air, broken only by the distant echo of fading spells and whispered anxieties from students behind Alden.

Almost as one, the other teachers—Evora, Tobin, Milena, Hugo—all turned their gazes toward Alden, their expressions clear in their message: he was the leader they had chosen—the one whose judgment they trusted above all others in this moment.

Alden paused for a single, heavy beat, feeling the weight of that silent nomination press upon him more heavily than any armor he had ever worn. He had spent years avoiding exactly this type of responsibility. He was content with simpler duties. Simpler problems. Now there was no avoiding it, and nowhere else to pass the burden.

He drew himself up fully as he slowly stepped forward into the space directly in front of the damaged barricade. Evora's shadows shifted around him protectively, and Tobin stood close behind, sword at the ready.

The man's gaze settled on Alden. His expression was neutral, betraying nothing. "And who might you be?"

"Alden Voss," Alden replied evenly, voice calm and unwavering, projecting clearly for all to hear. "I'm in charge here."

The man inclined his head slightly, a faint smile touching his lips—cold, controlled, calculating. "Lucian Vaelor. Pleased to make your acquaintance."

Alden frowned. "What do you want?"

"A conversation, Mr. Voss," said Lucian. "I believe we might resolve this without further violence."

Alden didn't trust that smile for an instant, but he held Lucian's gaze, measuring the danger carefully.

"You've already shattered our gates, attacked our academy, and terrorized our students," Alden replied, steel in his voice. "Forgive me if I find your claim of peaceful intent difficult to believe."

Lucian raised a single gloved hand, a gesture of calm. "We have specific objectives. Cooperate, and no one need be harmed."

Alden didn't reply immediately, letting the silence stretch. He knew every student, every teacher, every frightened soul behind him was listening and waiting for his response. This was his moment—the decision that could save them or doom them.

"Very well," he said finally, cautiously. "We'll talk. But understand me clearly: threaten these students again, and I'll see to it personally that you regret stepping foot inside these walls."

Lucian smiled slowly, darkly amused. "Excellent. I believe we understand each other perfectly."

CHAPTER THIRTEEN

Lucian Vaelor stood calm and composed in the fractured opening of the barricade. His cloak settled around his boots like smoke. The air between him and Alden crackled with the last vestiges of shattered wards and lingering shadow magic.

Inside, the cafeteria had gone silent—students clutched weapons they barely knew how to use. Teachers gripped their staves and blades with white knuckles. But all eyes were on Alden and the man who dared to demand a conversation after blasting open the gates.

Lucian offered a casual, almost amused nod toward the makeshift defenses. "You've held together well, all things considered. I expected more chaos. Fewer steel spines."

Alden didn't move. "You'll forgive us if we weren't eager to roll over."

Lucian smiled faintly. "It wasn't a criticism. I admire it, truly. Makes my job a bit more complicated, but there's honor in resistance."

"You didn't bring a war troll for an honorable conversation."

Lucian chuckled. "No. That was for the wards."

The statement hung in the air like a challenge. Alden let it sit, refusing to give Lucian the satisfaction of a reaction.

"Let's get to it," Alden said. "You didn't smash through our gates just to trade pleasantries."

Lucian's grin faded, but only slightly. "Very well." He took a slow step forward, just to the edge of the barrier. "We're here for one student. That's all. You hand him over, and we'll be on our way. No further damage. No unnecessary bloodshed."

Alden's shoulders tensed. "Who?"

Lucian's eyes gleamed. "Darion Valcroft."

A hush rippled through the cafeteria. Even behind Alden, he could hear it—the sharp intake of breath, the shuffling of students glancing toward each other.

Lucian went on, voice calm but cutting. "Darion is a valuable piece, you see. His father has coin. Power. Connections. And most importantly, the kind of pride that makes men do foolish things when family's involved."

"So you're here to kidnap the boy," Alden said flatly.

"'Kidnap' is such a *crude* word, Mr. Voss. We prefer the term 'strategic leverage.'" Lucian gestured vaguely toward the interior of the school. "Hand him over. We leave. No one else gets hurt."

Alden couldn't help the laugh that burst from him. It was low, rough, and hollow in the back of his throat.

"Let me get this straight," Alden said. "You thought you'd walk into a magic academy, point at a student—granted, a pompous little prick of a student—and we'd just hand him over to mercenaries to be ransomed like some sack of silver?"

Lucian's face didn't change, but his posture stiffened slightly.

Alden shook his head. "You've got the wrong school, Vaelor. We don't sell off our students. Not even the annoying ones."

Lucian's calm demeanor began to crack, if barely. "You misunderstand, Mr. Voss. I'm not *asking* you to like it. I'm offering you a choice. That one boy, or the deaths of every single being on these grounds." He swept his arm wide, gesturing toward the dozens of students behind Alden. "You think you can hold this line? Perhaps you can. *For a time.* But you're outmatched, outnumbered, and quite underprepared."

Murmurs stirred behind Alden. Fear, uncertainty, and the beginnings of panic.

Lucian's voice dropped, smooth and insidious. "This isn't heroism, Alden. It's pride. Pride that will get people killed."

Alden raised his hand behind him. The room went still again.

He took one step forward and let his voice rise—not angry, not panicked, just firm. Cold. Solid.

"You all listening?" he said, not taking his eyes off Lucian. "Good. Because I want this to be perfectly clear."

His voice rang through the cafeteria like iron striking stone.

"No life is more important than another. Not in this school. Not in this room. I don't care if Darion's an arrogant noble's son or a first-year with no magic to their name—no one gets handed over to these bastards to buy time."

He turned his head slightly, letting his voice carry to every corner. "Every single one of you is under our protection. And we don't sacrifice our own."

The murmurs stopped. Even the teachers, unsure just moments ago, stood a little straighter.

Alden looked back at Lucian. "You want him? Come take him. But you'll be going through me. And if I fall, there's another behind me. And another behind them."

He let that hang for several moments.

"But you better believe we protect our own," growled Alden.

Lucian's expression finally soured. His jaw tightened. "You're making a mistake."

"No," Alden said. "You did that when you came through that gate."

For a moment, neither man moved. The war troll behind Lucian shifted restlessly as its plated feet gouged deep furrows in the courtyard stone.

"So be it," Lucian said coldly. He stepped back, then blurred to the back line of his men.

He raised a gloved hand.

"Fire."

CHAPTER
FOURTEEN

The world lurched sideways.

A deafening roar split the air as a massive shockwave slammed into the shattered barricade, sending a concussive pulse rippling through the stone floor and every bone in Alden's body.

Explosions had thrown him off his feet countless times before, but this was different. This was raw power—concentrated and aimed with surgical precision.

The shadow barrier screamed under the impact. Evora staggered as shadows unraveled from her fingertips in uncontrolled tendrils. Tobin threw up his hands and cast a reactive ward, anchoring it just in time to prevent the front blast from vaporizing what remained of the cafeteria doors.

Alden had braced, instinctively raising his own fortification magic around his body—but it wasn't enough.

The force hit him square in the chest like a battering ram.

The impact ripped the air from his lungs. His boots left the ground. He flew backward, slamming into the floor and sliding across smooth stone until he collided with one of the cafeteria support columns.

The impact jolted through his spine, and for a moment, everything blurred.

Voices rang out—panicked, urgent—but they were muffled, as if submerged in water.

His vision snapped back into focus with a jolt of pain from his ribs.

He coughed once, sharp and dry, and forced himself to sit up.

A few students rushed toward him, wide-eyed and pale. One reached for his arm.

"Mr. Voss—"

"I'm fine," he growled, brushing them off as he pushed to his feet. His limbs ached, his back screamed, and a cut above his eyebrow was leaking blood into his eye—but he was on his feet. *That is what matters.*

His magic had done its job—just barely. The buffer had absorbed most of the impact, and turned what should've broken bones and crushed lungs into scrapes and bruises.

Alden wiped the blood from his brow with the sleeve of his shirt and looked to the front.

The barrier was still standing—but only just.

Evora was kneeling now, her hands pressed to the floor, sweat pouring down her face as she channeled everything she had into reinforcing the last remnants of her shadow veil.

Tobin stood behind her, sword in one hand, the other weaving precise gestures through the air, anchoring latticework glyphs into the space around the barrier. Each sigil pulsed once and locked into place like glowing, magical bolts.

Cracks lined the cafeteria's stone floor, and one window along the far wall had collapsed from the pressure of the blast.

Students huddled behind the overturned tables and benches. Some shielded others, but all of them were looking to the front with expressions ranging from terror to white-hot fury.

Milena sprinted toward the main line. Her raised hands were already glowing with heat and pressure as fire magic swirled at her fingertips like a barely contained storm.

"Whatever that was," she said, sliding to a halt beside Tobin, "they're not playing anymore."

"No," Tobin replied grimly, "they're not."

Alden limped back toward the front, shaking off the last of the impact. He moved with deliberate weight, like a statue coming to life, planting himself beside the teachers.

"Are we still breathing?" he asked.

Evora let out a weak laugh. "Barely."

"What the hell did they hit us with?"

Tobin didn't look away from the barrier. "Not a standard spell. Something custom. Focused. Probably some sort of siege-breaker enchantment."

Alden grimaced. "Effective, whatever it was."

More flashes lit the outside courtyard as the mercenaries regrouped. They hadn't charged in immediately. That worried him. They were testing the waters. Looking for weaknesses. That meant they weren't in a rush. They were confident.

"Status on the troll?" he asked.

Milena glanced toward the gap in the barricade. "It's in the back. Just standing there. Menacingly. I guess Vaelor's keeping it leashed... for now."

Alden nodded, then turned to the students closest to the front. "I need volunteers to help move the injured to the back. If you can't fight, that's fine. Help someone who can. Everyone else—stay low and wait for instructions. No panicking. Got it?"

A chorus of hurried nods followed.

Tristan was already halfway across the room. He took charge before Alden even had to ask. "You heard him. Let's go."

Alden turned back to the front just in time to see the first wave of mercenaries emerge from the smoke.

Five of them. And they were moving with practiced precision, flanking either side of the shattered entry. They drew their cloaks back. Their weapons glowed faintly with runes. They crept in slowly, probing.

"Here they come," Tobin muttered.

Evora pushed herself upright. "I've got enough left in me for one big trick. After that, I'll need cover."

"Make it count," Alden said.

He didn't have a sword. No shield. No armor.

But he had his fortification magic.

He had his instincts.

And he had something more dangerous than all of that—experience.

"Wait for my mark," he said.

Behind him, students were whispering to each other. Some were charging their own minor spells, while others steadied hands that trembled too much to hold makeshift weapons.

Alden stepped forward.

Closer to the broken threshold.

Closer to the mercenaries now approaching with slow, measured steps.

He could see Lucian in the distance, behind the ranks, still calm. Still watching.

Testing him.

Alden narrowed his eyes.

"You want to break us?" he muttered. "Let's see how many of you it takes."

CHAPTER
FIFTEEN

The first mercenary crossed the threshold and lunged at Alden with a sword sweeping high and fast—textbook killing strike.

Alden stepped into it.

He didn't parry. Didn't sidestep. He leaned in, brought his forearm up, and took the hit.

A metallic clang, like steel on stone, echoed as the blade slammed against his forearm. The attacker's eyes widened as the sword barely cut through the fabric of Alden's sleeve before glancing away. The force of the blow rippled across a thin shimmer of defensive magic embedded in Alden's skin like an invisible shell.

Alden grabbed the man's wrist, yanked him forward, and slammed a fist into his temple with all the weight of a stone wall behind it. Bone cracked. The man dropped like a sack of bricks. He was unconscious before his limp body hit the floor.

The next came with a spear—wider arc, meant to keep distance. Alden stepped past the thrust, grabbed the haft just behind the blade, and wrenched it sideways, pulling the mercenary off balance. Before the man could recover, Alden drove a knee into his stomach, then flipped him onto his back with practiced brutality. He stepped on the spear as it fell and kicked it back behind him—someone else could use it.

More were coming.

Three this time.

Alden exhaled slowly.

His skin shimmered faintly again as he drew from his well of fortification magic—just enough to harden his body like living armor. He didn't need to be fast. He just needed to endure long enough to return fire.

The first attacker struck low—a feint to the knee.

Alden took it on the thigh. The blade sparked as it scraped against enchanted muscle, glancing off with a hiss of magic and pain.

He grunted but didn't flinch.

His elbow shot downward like a hammer, catching the attacker at the base of the neck. The man crumpled.

The second tried to flank him—dagger in one hand, lightning spell charging in the other. That one Alden moved for, pivoting hard and slamming his forearm into the caster's wrist just as the spell released. The arc of electricity fired wide, crashing into the wall behind them and frying a tray of untouched food.

Alden stepped in and headbutted the man clean across the bridge of the nose. He collapsed with a wet grunt.

The third hesitated.

Big mistake. In war, hesitation gets you killed.

Alden closed the gap in two quick strides, grabbed the front of the merc's armor, and slammed him into the pillar he'd hit earlier. The man's head bounced off stone, and he dropped to the ground.

From behind the teachers' line, Milena loosed a wave of flame, forcing a pair of mercenaries back out of the breach. Tobin followed, sword crackling with raw force as he engaged the next wave before they could reform.

Alden's chest was heaving now. Sweat dripped down his

temples, and his knuckles were raw. Though his magic had absorbed most of the damage, it wouldn't last. His ribs ached from earlier. His muscles screamed from the constant strain of channeling fortification spells.

One of the mercs had taken a position on a knocked-over table and was chanting something Alden didn't recognize. Arcane circles formed beneath his boots—fast casting. It would be a heavy-hitter. A spell meant to clear the room.

Alden moved.

But not fast enough.

The spell flared to life—a cone of pure kinetic force, bursting outward in a roar. Alden couldn't dodge. He braced himself and poured the last of his current ward into his chest and shoulders.

The blast hit like a battering ram.

He staggered back, boots sliding across the blood-slick stone, and smashed into a support beam with enough force to crack it slightly. Pain exploded through his back, but he stayed upright.

Barely.

Blood spotted his lip. The merc was already charging again and was now wielding a shortsword. The man grinned.

"Voss!" Hugo's voice rang out from the kitchen.

Alden looked up just in time to see a blur of metal soaring through the air.

He caught it one-handed. It was heavy. Familiar. Unbalanced.

He grinned at the cast-iron frying pan. Its surface shimmered faintly with arcane etchings—the dull gleam of a durability enchantment pulsed across its weighty form.

"Oh, you beautiful bastard," he muttered.

The shortsword merc closed the distance.

Alden rose from his crouch and swung.

The pan struck the side of the attacker's head with a *THWACK* that echoed across the cafeteria like a gong. The enchantment flared on impact, and the man flew sideways, crashed through a bench, and didn't get back up.

A second mercenary froze mid-step. Alden turned his head toward him as blood ran down his cheek. The pan was still humming in his grip.

"Next," Alden said, eyes hard.

The merc backed away and ran out the door. *Smart man.*

Another came forward, thinking he could take Alden while he was still recovering. Alden spun the pan once in his grip and stepped in close. The man slashed with a dagger. Alden caught his arm, twisted, and brought the pan down onto the man's shoulder with a crack that made several students flinch.

The merc dropped like a sack of flour, screaming. Alden kicked him in the face and silenced him. He turned back toward the breach. The front line was collapsing under the sheer volume of pressure, and more attackers were pushing into the room.

Tobin held one of the lines with three older students. His sword danced through spells and steel with trained ease. Evora had collapsed to one knee again as her shadows flickered—but they were still active.

Milena shouted across the room, "They're flooding through the halls—we need a pushback now!"

Alden didn't wait for orders. He surged forward, frying pan raised, fortification magic lacing his arms once more.

The mercenaries hadn't expected a janitor to stand his ground.

They definitely hadn't expected a man to beat them to the floor with a pan.

CHAPTER
SIXTEEN

Alden was mid-swing—pan arcing in a wide, satisfying blur—when he caught the shimmer of magic gathering just off to his left.

Shit! Too late.

A sharp chant, clean and clipped, rang out. A burst of white-blue light erupted from the caster's outstretched palm and slammed into Alden's side like a cannonball. It didn't hurt exactly—it didn't need to. The moment it struck, the world twisted sideways and dissolved into darkness.

Not unconscious. Not exactly. Alden could feel his body—feel the ache in his limbs, the sweat on his skin—but the world around him had vanished. No light. No color. No form. Just a soundless void, thick as oil and cold as stone.

Then, faintly, the sound of battle returned—muffled, distant, like it was happening through several feet of water. Shouting, spells, the unmistakable thrum of metal on metal. The mercs were still advancing.

He heard a grunt. Tobin's voice, cursing.

Then footsteps. Closing.

Alden gritted his teeth. His vision was still gone, reduced to a black smear across his eyes, but he knew that sound. Three of them, maybe four. Coming fast. The caster who'd hit him must've used a veil spell—a cheap trick, designed to disorient and blind just long enough for a clean kill.

They thought they had him.

Wrong.

"Milo!" Alden shouted into the dark. "Milo, now—use your magic!"

There was no response. Just the continued crash of chaos and spells across the room. The enemy's footsteps were nearly on him now.

"Milo!" he bellowed again. "Use your damn spell—on the spellblades!"

Still no answer.

Alden swore. "Don't you freeze up on me now, kid! Hesitation kills!"

"I—I—yes, sir!"

The words came from across the room, high-pitched, frightened, but loud enough to cut through the noise.

Pop.

A soft shimmer touched the air—a ripple of arcane light that tickled Alden's skin like static. He couldn't see it, but he felt the effect. Milo had cast it.

Shining Veil was weak magic by most standards—barely enough to light a room, and all but harmless on its own—but Alden had seen what it did. It didn't blind. Didn't burn. It *revealed*. It highlighted outlines and made shapes visible even through illusion and shadow.

Suddenly, Alden could see.

Not with his eyes, but with a sense somewhere deeper. His vision hadn't returned, but in its place, he could make out three glowing silhouettes—bodies traced in dancing flecks of sparkling light.

They were less than ten feet away and closing fast.

Alden grinned.

"I see you."

The nearest mercenary hesitated. That was all the invitation Alden needed.

He stepped into the swing and brought the pan upward in a brutal arc that caught the lead attacker under the chin. The man's head snapped back and his feet lifted off the ground as he crashed hard onto the stone floor in a heap.

The second attacker shouted something—too slow. Alden twisted toward the new shimmer of light to his right and drove his elbow into the shape's midsection, feeling the satisfying crunch of armor denting under force. The merc folded forward, gasping.

Alden brought the pan around again. One clean strike to the back of the helmet. Another body down.

The third was smarter. He darted to the side, trying to flank—probably thinking that Alden's blind state was real. But Milo's magic still clung to him, lighting up the air around him like stardust in a wind tunnel.

Alden waited until the moment the sparkle paused—just enough hesitation in the merc's step—and moved.

He closed the distance in a burst of raw speed, reinforced by another surge of fortification magic. His shoulder slammed into the third merc's chest like a battering ram, driving the air from the man's lungs and hurling him backward into a toppled table.

The room exploded with noise again—students gasping, shouting, and several of them cheering.

Alden stood over the three fallen attackers, chest rising and falling like a piston, blood trickling from a shallow cut across his cheek. The pan hung loosely from one hand. His vision cleared.

"I said hesitation kills," he called out, turning back toward the room, voice booming.

A group of nearby students had gone deathly quiet. A few of them were still watching Milo, wide-eyed. One boy—older, smug—opened his mouth to say something about Milo.

"Try it," Alden warned, pointing at him with the pan. "You so much as smirk at that kid again, and you'll be joining the cleanup crew for the rest of the year."

The boy shut his mouth.

Milo, across the room, stood with both hands outstretched, the last motes of his magic fading from his fingertips. His face was pale, his breathing shallow, but his eyes... they were wide with something new. Something electric.

Pride.

Alden locked eyes with him and gave a single nod.

Milo straightened.

Another tremor shook the walls as the war troll outside bellowed. Dust fell from the rafters. The mercenaries hadn't finished yet.

But neither had they.

Tobin jogged over, face flushed, blade slick with ash and blood. "You good?"

Alden rolled his shoulder. "More or less. Milo saved my ass."

Tobin raised an eyebrow at the boy, impressed. "Didn't think that sparkle spell of his had any teeth."

"It doesn't," Alden replied, hefting the pan again with a smirk. "But it's one hell of a spotlight."

The pan vibrated faintly in his hand as another shockwave hit the outer barrier.

Alden turned back toward the shattered doorway, eyes burning.

"Now let's finish this."

CHAPTER SEVENTEEN

The cafeteria had become a war zone.

Smoke curled in lazy trails from scorched stone and shattered tables. The lingering stench of ozone mixed with blood and burnt wood as burn marks, left by misfired or deflected spells, lined the floor. Screams, shouts, and the hum of active magic filled the air.

Alden didn't have time to appreciate any of it. He was too busy smashing another mercenary across the jaw with the cast-iron pan.

The man spun and dropped like a sack of flour.

That made... what, six?

Maybe seven. He'd lost count after the third or fourth. Not that it mattered. They were still coming.

Another approached, this one wielding a short-handled war axe and a nasty grin. Alden ducked under the first swing, drove his elbow into the man's ribs, then twisted and brought the pan up under the attacker's chin. The merc's head snapped back, eyes rolling as he fell to the floor.

No time to breathe.

The last one of the current wave came at him fast—a woman,

slim and quick, twin daggers glowing faintly with enchantment. She feinted left, then slashed low. Alden blocked with the pan, sparks flashing on contact, then shoved her back with his free hand. She rebounded off a broken bench and lunged again.

Alden turned into the strike, letting one of the blades glance across his shoulder—his fortification magic dulled the edge to a shallow sting—and responded with a brutal hook of his own.

Pan met temple. The woman crumpled.

And then it was quiet.

For a moment.

He stood there in the middle of the cafeteria entrance, panting, clothes torn, blood soaking through the sleeve of his shirt. His magic was faltering—he could feel it—the layers of reinforcement thinning as the protective shell cracked like overused armor.

Across the rubble-filled hall, Lucian Vaelor stood watching.

He wasn't smiling anymore.

"Seven of my best," he said, his voice clear, magically enhanced again. "I paid good coin for them."

Alden spat blood onto the stone floor. "Should've asked for a refund."

Lucian's lips curled into something between amusement and irritation. "You know, I really did think this would be simpler. Break a few doors, flex some arcane muscle, collect the brat, and leave." He stepped forward, boots echoing sharply. "But no. You just had to be difficult."

Alden didn't respond. He was watching Lucian's hands. They were empty for now—but ready. Every movement was precise. Relaxed. *Controlled.*

Lucian stopped ten paces from him. "I'm growing tired of delays."

He reached into his coat and pulled out a slender dueling blade—not large, but long, elegant, and deadly. The edge glimmered faintly with runes.

"You've made your point," Lucian said, stepping into a ready stance. "But if you want something done right…"

He let the rest hang.

And then he lunged.

Alden just barely brought the pan up in time to deflect the first thrust. The clang rang through his bones.

Lucian flowed around his block, twisting into a wide arc, blade flicking out like a serpent. Alden blocked again—barely—but staggered under the force. Lucian pressed forward. His strikes were elegant and vicious as he danced around Alden's heavier, grounded style.

Alden fought back, hammering out wide arcs with the frying pan, trying to break Lucian's rhythm, but the man was fast—*too* fast. He ducked and weaved, slipping through narrow gaps. His blade carved out flickers of pain as it slipped past Alden's defenses again and again.

Alden grunted as another slash cut across his hip. He responded with a heavy backhand that would've crushed bone if it landed, but Lucian slid under it like water, as his blade flashed again.

"You're strong," Lucian said, circling. "I'll give you that. Tougher than you look. But slow."

Alden swung again. Missed.

Lucian punished him with a deep slash across the thigh. Alden stumbled.

"And tired," Lucian continued, calm and smug now. "You're bleeding. Breathing hard. That shielding of yours is cracking. You feel it, don't you?"

Alden straightened, sweat burning down his face. His chest heaved with every breath. His muscles screamed.

But he brought the pan up again.

"I feel it," Alden muttered. "Too damned old for this shit."

Lucian chuckled. "Indeed."

And then he lashed out with a spell—sharp and fast. A blast of kinetic energy erupted in his face, point-blank. Alden's weakened magic flared to life to try and absorb it, but it wasn't enough.

The force lifted him off the ground and hurled him backward like a ragdoll.

He crashed through a half-toppled bench, then hit the floor hard. He slid across the stone until he came to a stop just inside the cafeteria.

He didn't move.

For a long second, there was silence again.

Students stared, frozen. Even Tobin stopped mid-swing.

Alden lay there as the pan clattered from his hand and rolled in a slow circle beside him.

Lucian stepped through the breach in the barricade, eyes scanning the room like it already belonged to him.

"That," he said, voice smooth, "is how it ends."

Alden groaned, shifting slightly.

Not quite.

But close.

CHAPTER
EIGHTEEN

Alden couldn't breathe. Pain lanced through every rib as he lay sprawled on the floor. His chest rose and fell in shallow, ragged gasps. His arms wouldn't respond at first, and his vision blurred around the edges. He tried to roll onto his side and regretted it immediately.

Too old. Too damned broken.

His fortification magic had taken the brunt of Lucian's blast, but not all of it. The spell hit Alden, and he was sure something inside him had cracked—maybe a rib. Maybe more. He felt as if a grinder had mangled his arms and legs.

He heard shouting. The clash of steel. The hiss of spells.

Tobin's voice barked something from the front line. Milena let loose a burst of flame. Evora's shadows flickered erratically near the edges of the barrier. They were holding. Barely.

A *whomp*.

Followed by a pop, a crackle, and a hiss.

The scent hit him first—spice. Overpowering. Nose-burning. Sinus-destroying.

Something erupted at the front entrance—Alden forced his eyes open just in time to see Lucian stagger back, coughing violently and shielding his face as a haze of violently enchanted spice particles swirled around him. His dueling cloak flared, and his magical defenses struggled to compensate for the explosion of sensory overload.

Hugo stood behind a counter, one arm still extended, face grim.

"Crushed red sun peppers, powdered banshee root, and ghost fire salt," the cook said. "Been saving that one."

Lucian stumbled, retreating to the doorway, cloak sparking with active wards as he hissed and cursed under his breath. It wouldn't stop him for long—but it was enough.

Tristan's voice rose above the din. "Now! Everyone—focus on Mr. Voss! Buffs, shields, heals—anything you've got!"

The students responded without hesitation. Scared as they were, tired, burned, scraped and bruised—they obeyed.

Magic poured toward him.

Not in torrents or surges, but in hundreds of small, flickering sparks.

A warmth spread through Alden's chest first—a weak regeneration spell. Bones knitted, slowly. Bruises eased. The worst of the fire in his lungs subsided.

Something wrapped around his throat—not physically, but a magical weave—a ward to protect against silence and spell-locks. He felt his voice, his breath, his focus clear again.

A tingling around his fingers—a minor spell channeling boost.

His muscles eased under the press of a low-grade pain suppressant enchantment.

His boots grounded, then lightened as a mobility enhancement threaded into his steps.

Another spell tried to calm his racing heart, dulling the panic that had crept in at the edges. Focus enchantment—half-trained, probably botched in its casting—but it helped.

An overlapping shielding spell danced across his shoulders and arms, barely strong enough to stop a solid punch, but enough to buy him seconds.

Even his hearing cleared as someone managed a basic clarity charm, letting him pick out voices again from the noise.

None of them were strong. None of them were battlefield-grade.

But together—layered one over the other—they worked.

Alden rose.

First to one knee, then to his feet.

He stood straighter than he had in hours. His back still ached, his ribs still screamed—but now there was a buffer. Now there was strength.

He flexed one hand, and the magic didn't flicker—it held.

He looked toward the front, toward the entrance—Lucian had returned to the threshold. The spice haze was dissipating. The edge of his cloak was slightly torn. He looked pissed.

Lucian's eyes widened just slightly as he saw Alden stand, then narrowed. He chuckled.

"Well," he said, brushing his sleeve, "isn't that adorable."

He raised his voice, projecting for everyone to hear. "You're being propped up by children, Voss. Little leeches feeding you scraps of magic. You think that's strength?"

Alden took one step forward.

Then another.

He caught the pan from the floor as he passed it, rolling it once in his grip. The enchantments were still building.

"I think it's loyalty," Alden said, voice sharp now. Stronger. "I think it's courage."

He turned slightly, casting a glance back over his shoulder at the kids. "They stood when they could've run. They fought when they didn't have to. They chose to be here."

His gaze locked on Lucian. "Can you say the same about the people behind you?"

Lucian's eyes flashed. "This is pathetic."

Alden pointed the pan at him. "Then come and see what it gets you."

Lucian didn't wait.

He charged.

Their weapons met again in a clash of steel and iron. Sparks flew as runes collided. This time, Alden didn't stagger. He absorbed the impact and struck back. Lucian's blade danced, but Alden expected the rhythm now.

He moved faster—every buff helped. His swings were wider, heavier, and his timing sharper. Lucian's taunts faded into gritted teeth and focused breathing as the duel escalated.

They circled, blades struck again and again—Lucian was faster, more precise; Alden heavier, more brutal.

Lucian slashed toward Alden's legs. Alden jumped. His mobility spell gave him just enough height to avoid the arc.

Lucian spun with a follow-up, trying to cut across Alden's ribs.

Alden raised the pan like a shield. The blow hit hard—enough to jar his arm—but the enchantment held, and Alden didn't yield an inch.

A riposte. A shoulder check. A pan to the side of Lucian's head.

Lucian reeled.

A cheer broke out in the cafeteria.

Lucian's cloak lashed out magically, knocking Alden back a step. But Alden recovered and pressed forward, forcing Lucian to give ground for the first time since the battle began.

They were equals now. For the first time.

And the momentum was shifting.

CHAPTER NINETEEN

The clash of pan and blade rang out like thunder in the broken remains of the cafeteria. Alden pressed forward, ignoring the pain lancing up his arm with each swing. His breath came hard and fast as sweat dripped down his face, but he didn't stop.

Lucian parried another blow. He grit his teeth as Alden's enchanted frying pan slammed into his warded shoulder. His defenses flared in a burst of frustrated sparks.

"You're starting to look tired," Alden growled.

Lucian stepped back and dragged the back of his hand across his mouth where blood glistened at the corner. "You're supposed to be dead."

"Get in line," Alden said, and charged.

Lucian slashed low—Alden blocked with the pan, then caught Lucian's wrist with his free hand and twisted. Lucian hissed and countered with a point-blank burst of kinetic force. Alden was ready this time—he shifted his weight and let the spell roll over his enchanted frame. His boots skidded across the stone, but he kept his footing.

Behind him, students shouted—spells lit up the air in scattered bursts as they held off the few remaining mercenaries still inside the cafeteria.

Tobin and Milena had joined them at the front, pushing hard now that Lucian was distracted.

The tide is turning. Alden stepped in again and hammered the pan into Lucian's ribs with a crack that made the man stumble.

Lucian drew a dagger from his belt and lashed out in frustration, but Alden blocked it with his forearm. Blood bloomed across his skin, but his magic dulled the worst of the pain. He grabbed Lucian's wrist and slammed the man's hand into the wall, forcing the dagger to clatter to the ground.

Lucian roared and hurled a spell directly at Alden's face—a flash of searing white light.

Alden ducked and swung up. The edge of the pan caught Lucian across the jaw with a bone-jarring clang.

Lucian stumbled back, dazed, one hand raised to summon a fresh ward—yet Alden gave him no quarter.

He drove forward, bellowing, his pan raised high.

Lucian barely managed to intercept the blow, but the force of it shattered his ward like glass. His dueling blade snapped under the pressure.

He staggered, cloak torn, armor cracked, blood running freely down his temple.

Alden stood over him, chest heaving, pan in hand, ready for the final blow.

Lucian looked up, fury and disbelief etched across his face. "Y-you're just a janitor."

Alden wiped blood from his lip and grinned. "And I'm taking out the trash."

Lucian's hand clenched. A small crystal embedded in his palm pulsed.

"No!" Tobin shouted from behind. "He's teleporting—"

Light swallowed Lucian in a flash of silver-blue arcana, and then he was gone—vanished in a swirl of light and smoke.

The sound of the portal's collapse echoed through the ruined cafeteria.

And just like that... it was over.

The remaining mercenaries, suddenly leaderless, faltered. One dropped his weapon and ran. Another collapsed under a volley of stunning spells from Milena and the students.

The rest surrendered within seconds.

Alden stood there, shoulders slumped, weapon still raised.

Then the pan slipped from his fingers and clattered loudly to the floor.

He took one step back.

And collapsed.

His legs gave out entirely, and he dropped like a felled tree. The stone floor rushed up to meet him, and he only vaguely registered the students rushing forward.

He hit hard. Pain flared through his side. He groaned and blinked at the ceiling overhead as his vision spun. His magic was gone—completely depleted. Every nerve in his body screamed with fire.

Tobin knelt at his side in an instant. "Alden—hey—look at me."

"Already did my part," Alden mumbled. "Leave me for dead. Dramatic ending."

Tobin scoffed. "Don't be an ass."

Hugo arrived next, dropping to one knee with a bottle in hand. "Drink."

Alden sniffed it. "Smells like paint thinner."

"Either it'll fix your insides or finish the job. Either way, it'll be quiet."

Alden chuckled—and then coughed, which turned into a groan. He took a deep breath and chugged the thick, red liquid. Warmth spread through his body as the healing potion began to take hold. His eyelids became even heavier and drooped.

Students gathered around, crowding close, whispering with wide eyes and trembling hands.

Milo appeared among them, bruised and scuffed, but beaming. "You did it, Mr. Voss."

Alden blinked up at him. "No, kid. We did it."

And then the pain caught up to him all at once.

He closed his eyes and passed out cold.

CHAPTER TWENTY

The morning sun filtered softly through the infirmary's high, arched windows, casting golden light over rows of quiet cots and shelves stacked with glass bottles, bandages, and strange glowing salves. Most of the beds were empty now. The battle was days behind them, and things had slowly begun to return to some semblance of order.

Alden grunted as he swung his legs off the edge of the cot. His ribs still ached, but the healers had done their work well. *Real* healers. The kind that didn't burn your skin off while trying to knit it back together.

The head healer—a stern woman with silver hair and no tolerance for nonsense—stood nearby with her arms folded. Deep lines creased the corners of her eyes, etched from decades of squinting at injury reports and obstinate patients.

Her robes were utilitarian, dark green with pale gold trim, every hem pressed and clean despite the chaos of the infirmary. A long scar traced down one cheek, a silent testament to a past that no one dared to ask about. Her eyes were sharp as a scalpel. They swept over

Alden like she was diagnosing half a dozen new problems just by looking at him.

"You're lucky you only cracked three ribs, strained half your body, and walked away with a minor concussion. I'd say 'take it easy,' but I've met you."

Alden rolled his shoulder and winced. "Pain's a good reminder that I'm still alive."

"Keep talking like that and I'll keep you another week."

He raised his hands in surrender and slid off the bed. "No offense, ma'am, but I've had enough potions and poultices shoved down my throat to last the year."

She smirked and handed him his coat. "Out, then. Don't make me regret it."

He nodded, thanked her in his own gruff way, and limped down the corridor toward the staff lounge, where voices buzzed like hornets behind the closed door.

The senior staff had returned.

He pushed open the door.

It was chaos.

Professors and instructors argued over broken ward lines, destroyed corridors, and damaged infrastructure. Magical charts floated in midair, held aloft by projection glyphs, displaying the structural damage to every wing of the academy. The center of it all stood Dean Albrecht Vayne, grim-faced, arms crossed behind his back as he listened to two instructors argue over blame.

When Alden entered, the room went quiet for just a second too long.

Then Dean Vayne turned to him. "Ah. Mr. Voss. I trust your time in the infirmary was productive?"

"You could say that." Alden crossed the room slowly, eyeing the destroyed campus map. "Looks like you missed a hell of a party."

Vayne's jaw tightened. "We received your missives after the fact. By then, our assignment had us too far afield to return in time."

Alden folded his arms. "Right. Convenient."

"You have something to say, Mr. Voss?"

"Yeah." Alden stepped forward, meeting the Dean's gaze. "Next time you decide to gallop off on a secret mission with every heavy-hitter in the building, maybe leave a little more than a skeleton crew behind. Unless, of course, you're planning on leaving the fate of your students to the janitor again."

Gasps rippled across the room. Tobin raised an eyebrow but said nothing. Evora looked positively delighted.

Vayne's lips thinned. "That skeleton crew held the line."

"Barely." Alden gestured toward the map. "We had a war troll in the courtyard. Spellblades inside the walls. The only reason this place is still standing is because the *kids* decided they weren't going to die quietly."

"And because of you," came a voice from the far side of the room.

Everyone turned as Archduke Rendell Valcroft stepped forward from the shadowed alcove near the fireplace, hands clasped behind his back, his expression unreadable.

Vayne bowed slightly. Alden didn't move.

The Archduke's gaze lingered on him. "My son was nearly taken. He was humiliated. Threatened. Injured. And forced to hide behind overturned tables like a common orphan."

Alden's fists clenched, and he took a breath to reply—

"But," Valcroft continued, "he is alive. Because of you. Because of all of you."

Silence. Alden blinked.

"I have read every report. I've spoken to the students. I know what happened here. You stood between my son and death, Mr. Voss. You and your staff—and your students—held against impossible odds. For that, I am in your debt."

He paused, his eyes sweeping across the stunned room.

"And it is my sincere hope," he added, "that we can all look forward to what Warden's Rest will accomplish in the coming years. This place—this school—has produced more heroes in one night than I've seen in a decade of courtly pretense."

Before Alden could process that, the Archduke turned to the Dean. "And as for Mr. Voss..."

Alden's eyes narrowed. "I'm good, thanks."

"Nonsense," Valcroft said smoothly. "For your service, your valor, and the disturbingly effective use of a kitchen implement, you are hereby promoted to Strategy and Defense Instructor of Warden's Rest Academy."

A few teachers clapped. Evora grinned. Tobin's laughs turned into a guffaw.

Alden sighed, dragging a hand down his face. "This a paid promotion, or just more work?"

"Both," Vayne said, clearly enjoying this now. "You'll be teaching twice a week, overseeing practical defense training, and running emergency drills."

"Great," Alden muttered. "More children. With weapons."

CHAPTER
TWENTY-ONE

The morning sun crept slowly over the spires of Warden's Rest, casting long shadows across the scarred cobblestone paths and the battered facade of the academy's east wing. A cool breeze stirred through the air, carrying with it the faint scent of ash, fresh-cut stone, and wet mortar.

Alden stood alone on the training grounds, arms crossed, eyes tracing the lines of cracked walls and half-repaired fences. Hammers rang in the background, joined by the occasional burst of arcane light as mages carefully resealed wards and rethreaded enchantments into the school's damaged infrastructure.

It had only been a few days, but the place already looked more alive than it had in years. Perhaps because, for the first time, the students had fought for it.

He took a deep breath, savoring the crisp air. His ribs still twinged, and his shoulder bore a tightness that the healers promised would fade eventually. The fatigue, the weight behind his eyes, the echoes of screams and fire and steel—those would linger longer.

He glanced to his right, where a chunk of the training yard wall had been replaced with mismatched stones. The work was temporary—a patch job, but it stood solid and reliable.

Like most of the people who'd defended this school.

He let out a slow breath. "Too old for this shit."

The words came easier now like a grim sort of mantra. He still meant them. But for the first time in a long while, he didn't say it with regret.

Behind him, the soft sound of footsteps on stone drew his attention. He turned to see Evora approaching, her coat buttoned against the wind, her hair braided neatly behind her shoulders.

"Thought you might try to disappear before your first lesson," she said.

"Tempted," Alden replied. "Still not convinced this isn't some elaborate punishment."

Evora smiled faintly. "You'll be brilliant at it. Whether you like it or not."

She gestured toward the far end of the field, where students were beginning to gather—some chatting nervously, others already sitting in rows with notebooks open.

Alden's brow rose slightly. "They're early."

"They're *eager*," Evora said. "You gave them something worth believing in. Don't downplay it."

Alden scratched his chin, feeling the faintest itch of stubble. "It was a hell of a week."

She nodded. "And now you get to help them prepare for the next one."

He watched as the students settled in, surprised to see how many were present. Milo sat at the very front, hands folded neatly over an empty notebook, his expression determined. Tristan was beside him, his uniform crisp, gaze sharp and alert.

And beside them sat Darion Valcroft. His posture was rigid and a new quill was gripped tightly in his hand. He nodded to Alden as their eyes met—not as a nobleman acknowledging a subordinate, but as a student acknowledging a teacher.

That one still caught Alden off guard.

Evora gently nudged his shoulder. "They're waiting."

He grunted. "Still have time to fake my death."

"Go," she said with a smirk. "Or I'll start your lesson for you."

Alden stepped forward. His boots crunched lightly on the gravel path as he made his way toward the front. The sounds of construction still echoed around the academy, but quieter now. Focused. Purposeful.

The same could be said for the students.

He stopped at the center of the field, facing them. A long wooden rack stood behind him, stocked with practice weapons—staves, shields, dull blades enchanted to resist causing real injury. His old jacket hung open at his sides, and though the cast-iron pan was not currently on his belt, the rumor of it had clearly reached the first-years. A few whispered and nudged each other excitedly when he stepped into view.

He said nothing at first and simply let the silence stretch. The sun peeked out from behind a cloud, lighting the field with soft gold.

He looked at Milo, who sat like a statue—ready.

He looked at Darion, whose eyes never wavered.

He looked at Tristan, who nodded once—the way soldiers used to nod before battle.

Alden cleared his throat.

"I'm not your usual instructor," he said. "I'm not going to show you how to wave a wand with flair or win points in a tournament."

He let that settle.

"I'm going to teach you how not to die. Everyone here has had first-hand experience in what *exactly* I mean by this."

A few students shifted uncomfortably. Others leaned forward, riveted.

"I'm going to teach you what it means to stand between danger and the people who can't fight for themselves. I'm going to show you how to hold the line when no one else will. Because whether you like it or not—whether you ever see combat or not—you're going to be part of something bigger than yourself."

He started to pace slowly in front of the rows.

"Some of you are nobility. Some of you aren't. That doesn't matter in the *slightest*. When the walls break and fire rains from the sky, titles will *not* protect you. What will protect you, however, are the people standing at your side."

A few students looked at each other, surprised. More than one pair of eyes flicked toward Milo.

Alden stopped pacing and turned to face them again.

"You're here because this academy survived a siege. Because *you* survived a siege. You've already done what half the nobles in this kingdom wouldn't have the guts to do. And now we will build on that."

He straightened his shoulders.

"We'll start simple. Body positioning. Movement. Balance. You're going to learn how to fall without breaking something and how to get back up when you *do* fall."

He paused. His thoughts drifted back to the hundreds of recruits he had trained in the past. A thousand days like this on far-off training fields. Then he looked at them again—The scared, the hopeful, the wide-eyed, and the eager.

He smiled, just a little.

"Alright," Alden said. He took a deep breath and let it out. "Lesson one..."

The shenanigans continue in
Field Tripped
Episode Two of The Keepers of Warden's Rest

A NOTE FROM THE AUTHOR...

Hopefully, you've enjoyed this story as much as I enjoyed writing it. I'm really looking forward to writing the rest of The Keepers Of Warden's Rest!

If you would be so kind as to take a moment and leave a review, I would be extremely grateful. Reviews are the only real way for new, self-published authors to be seen on Amazon, so your positive comments will help immensely.

Feel free to visit my website to sign up for the reader group to receive updates on upcoming releases, as well as receiving our "starter library", a collection of prequel novellas for each series, as they become available.

— JEREMY FABIANO

About the Author

Information Security Analyst by day, father and creator by night.

Jeremy Fabiano is an emerging author of several exciting genres, which include: LitRPG, Fantasy, Science Fiction, Post Apocalyptic, Medieval Post Apocalyptic, and Non-Fiction.

Join him as he descends into the depths of his imagination, bringing you the exciting adventures he discovers along the way.

Jeremy Fabiano read his first fantasy book at fourteen years old. An old ratty copy of "The Hobbit." Tolkien forever dominated his imagination as he fell prey to every RPG game out there.

At sixteen, a friend from school introduced him to his first multiplayer RPG: A M.U.D. or multi-user dungeon. This ancient construct required the player to use a terminal program to connect to a remote text-based system. No pictures. No animations. It paved the way to being enthralled by World of Warcraft, where he saved the world countless times over the span of half of a decade.

In mid-2018, he reached out to several authors seeking advice. Shayne Silvers was among the first to respond. He encouraged and inspired Jeremy to work harder than he ever had before. Shortly after, M. D. Massey also gave some much-needed advice, eliciting even more changes in the aspiring author.

By the end of 2018, he had teamed up with T.M. Edwards and co-authored "Roger" - a book in Edwards' "Tales Of Courage From Beyond The Apocalypse" series. This would be the first of many books published by Jeremy Fabiano.

Keep reading. Keep learning.
Never be afraid to reach for your dreams

To get in touch:
www.jeremyfabianoauthor.com
www.amazon.com/author/jeremyfabiano

facebook.com/JeremyFabianoAuthor
x.com/jeremyfabiano
instagram.com/jeremyfabianoauthor

Acknowledgments

Words cannot express my gratitude. But, I'll attempt it anyway...

There's an old saying which I'm going to carelessly steal half of: It takes a village.

Writing a book does indeed take a village. And I'd like to thank some of those wonderful people who made my dream a reality. The people below have supported in one way or another throughout the entire project. From writing advice to marketing theory, from reality-checks to late-night conversations that last until sunup, you are the reason this book is possible.

Shayne Silvers. I've loved your stories from the get-go and can't wait to catch up on the latest. Thank you for always pushing me to do better. For never letting me be mediocre and complacent. I might not have had the balls to go forward with this project if you hadn't believed in me and encouraged me to do better.

 My *World of Warcraft*© friends: Heather, Brad, Doug (and his wife Becky). Thank you all for the wonderful adventures we've shared and continue to share. I was more than happy to create characters based on your toons in homage to our shenanigans and friendship.

There's a whole slew of others that won't fit on these pages, but need mentioning in no particular order. M.D. Massey, Ian Lahey, R.L. King,

Edward Brody, Jennifer Stowers. There's a ton more, but I can't remember them off the top of my head. I apologize for anyone I might have missed.

—JEREMY FABIANO

Made in the USA
Monee, IL
14 September 2025

24941762R00069